LABYRINTH

DEUCES WILD BOOK THREE

ELL LEIGH CLARKE

MICHAEL ANDERLE

DISRUPTIVE IMAGINATION

LMBPN Publishing
PMB 196, 2540 South Maryland Pkwy
Las Vegas, NV 89109

First US edition, September 2018
Version 1.01, February 2019

LABYRINTH TEAM

Thanks to the JIT Readers

John Ashmore
Peter Manis
Kelly O'Donnell
Kim Boyer
Daniel Weigert
Larry Omans
Micky Cocker
Larry Westman

If I've missed anyone, please let me know!

Editor
Lynne Stiegler

Rebus Quadrant, Themis Colony, Mess Hall

Nickie waited in the dinner line with Grim. The day's labor had taken it out of them both, and Grim was leaving Nickie to her thoughts while the line shuffled forward.

She was still finding her feet as someone who gave a shit. It was an entirely different mindset to the one-woman universe she'd lived in before her special functions had been activated. Not so long ago she had been free, fighting her way around the galaxy, unburdened by purpose or responsibility.

Or sobriety.

She had been...

Lonely. You were lonely, Nickie.

Nickie made a face and sighed. *I wish I could argue with you there.*

Shall I give you a moment to think it over? I am certain you can find something to disagree with.

Bitch. She reached the head of the line and greeted

Melissa, who was in charge of this communal meal, with a smile.

These last few weeks on Themis had reminded Nickie what it was like to be part of a community. Part of a family. She was finally beginning to flirt with the possibility that letting people in did not automatically mean they would leave, but she wasn't quite ready for her real family. Not yet.

People were still a pain in the ass, especially since part of her still craved the ease of losing herself to the party. It was simple to just give up responsibility for herself, to numb that deep ache of loss. But it wasn't *that* bad having people around. At least, there were some aspects she was getting used to. Getting fed was one of the pluses.

She held her tray up to accept Melissa's offering.

Grim gave her a little nudge with his tray and nodded toward Adelaide.

Nickie narrowed her eyes at the slumped shoulders and the desultory way she picked at her food. Adelaide spotted them and brightened immediately. She waved cheerfully at Nickie, who met Adelaide's sweet smile with one of her own and made her way over to the table.

This is personal growth, Nickie. I'm impressed.

Nickie snorted, then blushed when the people around her laughed good-naturedly. They'd all gotten used to her sporadic bursts of laughter and the occasional comment aloud to Meredith. *What the fuck does an EI know about growth?*

I know you would have turned around and walked away from this not so long ago. You are learning to care for these people.

I wouldn't go that far, although I do kind of like it here. It's out of the reach of my family, and frankly, these people need my help. They're just gonna keep getting picked off by whatever Skaine come by, and I never mind dealing with those fuckers. She nodded at Keen, who nodded back and returned to his conversation. *Besides, it might not necessarily be a bad thing to care.*

Will wonders never cease? Perhaps next we can work on caring about yourself, if that is not a step too far?

Don't push it.

Nickie took a seat on the bench next to Adelaide, and Grim chose the empty space across from her next to Keen. Raynard was conspicuously absent, and Nickie raised an eyebrow at the slight shadow under Adelaide's eyes.

Adelaide was getting used to Nickie's unasked questions. "I'm okay, honest. Just tired from construction on the water supply line. Where's Durq?"

Grim nodded toward the door. "He went back to his quarters for some quiet time. He worked with the planters all day today."

"Oh, I see." Adelaide grinned, then pressed her lips together to hide the small smile. "They're a little chatty, that's for sure. I had a visit from Leesha and Roan this afternoon."

Keen's bushy eyebrows knitted together in mild surprise. "Oh? What did they want? I can believe Leesha was there distracting you, but it's not like Roan to leave during the shift."

Adelaide stirred her food. "They wanted to talk about the best place to situate the mains access once we get the pipe run over from the reservoir. And for me to put in a word with you about getting a little more water from the reserves in the meantime."

Keen sighed. "I hope you're getting somewhere with that, Addie. Our water reserves are starting to run low." He put his spoon down and pushed his tray away. "We have enough for now," he told them, "but we need to get the desalination plant working and finish running the supply line out to the dome if we're going to meet the colony's agricultural needs."

Nickie lifted an arm. "It'd also be good to get off rationing and have a real fucking shower. The sonic shower just lacks something, you know?" She shifted in her seat and took a hasty bite of her food. Having a wet shower would be nice. She waved her fork at Keen as she continued, "The climate control installation was completed today. As soon as the water tanks are at capacity, the environmental systems can be brought online, and the agricultural workers can expand production. I can't believe you guys had all that equipment just gathering dust in storage."

Keen shrugged in resignation. "It wasn't exactly an option. We've been a little preoccupied with being raided by every passing contingent of Skaine until you got here."

Adelaide patted Keen's hand and pushed his tray back toward him. "Eat up. You need your strength." Her ponytail swished as she lifted her chin and put a finger up to silence his protest. "I don't care if you *want* to eat, you *need* to. None of us have had time to grieve. We're all dealing with it by pulling together and rebuilding."

Keen picked up his spoon, muttering under his breath.

Nickie snickered. "So, Adelaide, how long until the water is running?"

Adelaide pressed her lips together and tilted her head side-to-side while she did the calculations. Finally, she held up her hands and shrugged. "Um, I can't really be sure. We're learning as we go, and since we lost both of our engineers in the Skaine attack, we're relying on the manuals in the database to teach us how to do most of it." She smiled brightly at Nickie. "Actually, the interface you provided with Meredith has been incredibly helpful while everyone is getting used to their new roles."

Nickie's heart dropped.

Are you going to start blaming yourself again? Meredith asked.

Shut up, *Meredith!*

Adelaide noticed the drop in Nickie's mood. "What is this, brooders' corner? You're as bad as Keen! You can't keep blaming yourself, Nickie. You've worked harder than anyone here these last few weeks, and we all appreciate it. *You* didn't invite the Skaines over to kill our support personnel. Give yourself a break."

Nickie pushed her tray away and made a show of yawning. "Well, tomorrow holds another full day of work. I've got a couple of things to do, and then I'm going to hit the sack." She stood and slapped Grim on the back. "I'll see you in the morning, bright and early."

Grim looked up from his conversation. He took in the careful way she held her face and nodded. "Call if you need me, okay?"

Nickie nodded tightly and left.

Adelaide rolled her eyes and turned to Grim. "She didn't hear a word of that, did she?"

Grim shrugged. "She's a smart woman. It'll sink in…eventually."

Nickie made her way to her quarters without stopping to talk when Durq popped his head out of his room. She closed the door behind her, then flung herself face down on her bed and screamed soundlessly into her pillow.

Meredith remained silent, allowing Nickie the space to vent her grief and frustration.

Eventually, Nickie sat up. She clutched the pillow to her chest and leaned back against the wall with her eyes closed. "Why does everything have to *hurt* so damn much?"

I was once told that life is pain, and you have to grab the joy from it before it escapes or be lost to despair.

Nickie opened her mouth to argue. *I…can't disagree. Fuck, that's twice in one day. Am I sick?* She put a hand to her forehead and snickered. *I must be sick. Are my nanos malfunctioning?*

Funny! My point remains. Not only are you not *responsible for the deaths of the colonists, but you have also gone out of your way to ensure they are taken care of. You have nothing to feel guilty about.*

I wasn't going to just leave them to fucking die, and believe me when I tell you they all would have died if I hadn't intervened. Now that they have the defenses up and running, they can get this place thriving like it was supposed to in the first place. She threw the pillow back to its place and got up from her bed. "I need some thinking time."

You mean you need to hit something.

Nickie smirked. *Same thing.*

She pulled out a drawer and emptied the contents on her table, then began to organize the pile. She placed the already completed part to the side and organized the rest to remind herself what she had to work with. *Besides, it's the activity itself that counts right now. I need to occupy my hands.* She picked out a long, curved sewing needle and a thick ball of bonded nylon thread.

Craft projects are a well-documented method of therapy, Meredith offered. *Perhaps this will help clear your mind.*

Craft, my ass. Nickie snorted as she tied the ends of the coated thread off after threading the needle. *I have something a bit more physical in mind to burn off this frustration.* She sorted through the materials on the table and selected a rectangular piece and a long strip of material, which she pinned inside-out to one edge of the larger piece. *A clear mind would be good.*

Nickie picked up the sewing needle and started to stitch the two pieces of material together. "But first I have to work on letting this guilt go and learn to grab joy by the balls before it escapes."

Rebus Quadrant, Themis Colony, Airfield

Nickie strode determinedly up the ramp of the *Penitent Granddaughter* and headed straight for the cargo hold they'd never used. The only things in the open area were a weight bench and a big pile of rags on the floor near the door.

Her eyes widened at the size of the rag pile. She'd asked Durq to find her something to stuff her homemade punching bag with and it looked like the little Skaine had dug up every scrap of cloth on the ship.

She sniffed.

He'd even washed them for her. "Aw, Durq," she muttered. She sat cross-legged on the floor beside the pile and unpacked the sack and a flat, heavy disc from her carryall.

You're growing attached to him.

Nickie couldn't prevent the grin that broke out. *I know, right? It's fucking weird. It's like he's so vulnerable it cancels out all the parts of me that want to smash his Skaine face in.*

Charming.

Nickie shrugged and grabbed a handful of rags. *What? Don't judge me. It's the truth.* She stuffed in a layer of rags and then placed the weighted disc on top before snatching another handful of rags for the next layer.

It is?

Nickie rolled her eyes. *Durq is okay. Not just for a Skaine, but actually okay as a person.* She packed the rags in until the bag was full, keeping a close eye on the seams to check for splits before she threaded the tie in at the top. *Who'd have thought anyone could like a Skaine?*

She picked the bag up to test the weight. "Shit, this is a lot heavier than I expected." She bounced the bag in her hand a couple of times and nodded with satisfaction when the tie held. "Now, which beam is gonna hold this?" She dropped the punching bag gently and removed a long chain with a metal clip on each end from her carryall.

Nickie glanced at a girder that looked wide and thick enough. She coiled the long chain and held it loosely in one hand while she tossed the end over the top of the beam.

She missed the first time, but her second attempt was successful.

She caught the end of the chain as it fell and threaded it through the tie, then began to haul the heavy bag up one pull at a time.

You have a message.

"Huh?" The distraction caused the chain to slip through Nickie's hands. The bag plummeted, and the chain bit the skin of her fingers. "Shit!" She caught the chain before the bag hit the floor.

Meredith's tone was dry. *A message, Nickie. You have one.*

Ignore it, Mere. I'm too busy. She paused to wipe the sweat from her eyes and recommenced pulling the chain hand-over-hand until the bag was at the perfect height. A thought occurred to her. *Who the fuck even knows where I am to send a message?*

I wouldn't know. The message is from an anonymous sender.

It's probably spam. Or a scam. Nickie grunted as she anchored the chain to a support column. *Or,* she snickered, *it might be my lucky day, and it's a dick pic from a disaffected Torcellan noble who just needs me to send him twenty thousand credits so he can cross space to rock my world.*

You would know who sent the message if you read it.

Nickie smirked as she stood back to admire her work. *Was that almost a chuckle? Well, that's a relief. I was starting to think your sense of humor didn't make it into this version of you.*

Silence from Meredith.

Oh, fine, if it will make you happy then put it up on my HUD. Here's hoping it's the di— Oh. Oh no. No. Fuck that.

What is the issue? It is a simple request for assistance.

Nickie's lip curled. *It's a fucking babysitting job, that's* what. *Some overindulged royal sweetheart's gotten himself lost on sabbatical, and his family wants someone to go and hold his overly soft hand while he fucks about doing whatever it is princes do.*

Meredith tsked. *That is not what the message says. The prince has gone missing while on tour, and the royal family is in fear for his safety.*

Nickie grabbed the roll of tape she'd brought and got to work wrapping her hands. *You have to read between the lines, Mere. Look, John Deblanc of Zuifra, right?* She tore the tape with her teeth and smoothed the end down over her knuckles.

It is.

And what stands out about that message?

It is a human planet, one of the ones who chose a monarchy to govern when the colony was founded. But there are plenty of human planets who chose that model, Nickie. Meredith went quiet for a moment. *Oh. I see what you mean.*

Nickie jabbed lightly at the bag to test it. *"I see what you mean?" Our missing Prince John is on a quest. A fucking quest, Meredith.* She grimaced at the cuteness of it all and hit the bag a little harder. *Like a damn fairy tale.*

I was referring to the markers which indicate the message was transmitted using Federation technology.

Nickie paused mid-punch. *It was what? Are you fucking joking?*

I thought my information was clear.

Nickie sighed. *It was. You know what this means though, don't you?*

That someone in the Federation knows where to find you.

That someone in the Federation knows where to find me, she echoed. *No shit, but how? We're all the way out past the frontier. We shouldn't be within range of Federation communications.*

She stepped up the pace of her punches, finding comfort in the rhythm as she worked through her techniques. As always, she made it a point not to examine exactly why she found such peace in an activity she'd railed against in her youth.

"And besides, I only have two years left before I get dragged back to the Federation. Aunt Bethany Anne wants me to find myself, but how the fuck am I supposed to do that if they won't leave me the fuck alone to fucking *think?*"

She punctuated the last with a backfist but forgot to pull it. The bag split with a dull rip, spilling its innards.

"Dammit!" Nickie examined the split seam with a sigh. "Whatever. I'm not in the mood to train now, anyway."

What's really got you so riled? Meredith asked.

Nickie unwound the chain and lowered the bag to the floor. *What's got me riled is that whoever sent this thinks they can just snap their fingers and I'll come running.* She propped the bag against the weight bench and made a face at the split. *Well, they can all fuck themselves, I'm not doing it. And if the Federation wanted me, then they shouldn't have sent me away in the first place. The prince's family can find someone else to save their royal asses.*

Nickie left the hold and made her way to her quarters. She skirted Lefty and Bradley in the main corridor. "You two together again?" she asked the bots. "People are going to start talking, you know."

The bots made no reply, which suited Nickie just fine. She arrived at her quarters. The moment she closed the door behind her, she dumped the punchbag and the carryall in a corner and flopped into the chair to unlace her boots.

Are you okay?

She kicked her boots off and grabbed a set of clean clothes from the drawer. *I'm too tired to work it out now. I'm gonna take a shower and hit the sack.*

Meredith kept a close watch on Nickie's emotional state while she waited for her to finish the shower. Her concern was that Nickie's natural instinct to retaliate against perceived pressure would cause her to slip back into her old ways. She'd shown a little of it in her reaction to the message. Meredith knew Nickie would do the right thing since it was in her DNA, but Nickie had to come to that conclusion herself.

Maybe not completely alone, though.

She waited until Nickie emerged from the bathroom. *Nickie, would you look at that! The time lock just expired on the next entry from your aunt's diary.*

Nickie dropped the dirty clothing she was carrying into the laundry hamper and headed for her bed. She lay back and folded her arms behind her head with a smile.

Show me the entry, Meredith.

CHAPTER 2 TABITHA

Yollin System, QBBS *Meredith Reynolds*, Rangers' Area, Meeting Room

Tabitha, Hirotoshi, and Ryu sat across the table from Barnabas while Tabitha filled in some of the blanks in her after-action report. Bethany Anne had ordered their return to the *Meredith Reynolds* after the mission on Flex, and they'd arrived earlier and gone straight to the Rangers' area where Barnabas was waiting.

Tabitha leaned toward Barnabas. "So then, Ryotoshi—"

Barnabas shook his head in exasperation. "Tabitha." He gave her a stern look across the table, then glanced at Hirotoshi and Ryu. The Tontos gave deliberate identical shrugs, much to Tabitha's annoyance.

They had kept this up since Flex, simply because they knew it annoyed the hell out of her.

"You see what I have to deal with," she told Barnabas. "Anyway, Ryo*toshi*," she repeated, "starts shaking his ass in the middle of the circle like he was born for it, and I almost spat my drink all over the Torcellan noblewoman. Luckily for me, I was in complete control, even though the disguise I was wearing made me look like a sack of potatoes."

Barnabas furrowed his brow at Hirotoshi, who gave a minute shrug. "I fail to see what bearing your attire had on the situation."

Tabitha tilted her chair and put her feet up on the table. "Only *everything*. It was a public disservice. I nearly walked out until I saw that the other women were even more frumpily dressed than I was."

"But you are a Ranger," Barnabas pointed out, "not a model. Perhaps you took a knock to the head that left you confused as to the difference between the two professions?"

Ryu snorted softly.

Tabitha's mouth quirked. "I don't know why you're laughing, Ryu. You looked like a peacock in that Torcellan getup."

Ryu just smirked.

"Fine." She smirked back, extra-smirkily. "Don't say a word. I'll talk for you. 'May I have a thousand push-ups, Ranger Tabitha?' Why, of *course* you may, Ryu. It would be my pleasure to order them."

"It is your prerogative." Ryu's smirk deepened. "*I* did not have the most outrageous 'look' that night, did I, Kemosabe?"

Tabitha glared at Ryu. "I have *no* idea what you're talking about."

Ryu lifted an eyebrow. "But your description on the rooftop was so...detailed."

Tabitha's eyes widened as she tried to push the image away before—

"Oh, good God, *no*." Barnabas moaned. "Tabitha, why?"

"I promise I was not the one who started that." Tabitha took one look at the pained expression on her mentor's face. "Oh, lighten up. You've never wondered what you'd look like with tatas?"

Barnabas groaned and held his head in his hands. "No, Tabitha. I haven't."

Her shoulders shook with laughter, and she almost lost her balance as Barnabas' face worked through a series of emotions, none of them positive.

She pulled herself together with difficulty. "Well, at least now you know the leather-pants look isn't for you, so really, I did you a favor. You should be thanking me."

They were interrupted by the arrival of Bethany Anne and John. John waved at Tabitha and pulled the door closed, remaining outside.

"Sorry. I'm running over today." The Empress slapped Tabitha's feet off the table as she breezed past to get to her seat.

Tabitha stuck her tongue out at Ryu for snitching while Bethany Anne exchanged a brief greeting with Barnabas.

Tabitha went to put her feet back up, but Bethany Anne's expression told her not to push it. "Good to see you, but what was so urgent you called us all the way home? Couldn't spend another day without me, huh?"

Bethany Anne's mouth twitched. "Yes, Tabitha, I called you back from the ass-end of the Empire just so I could see your face. That would be a *fantastic* use of my resources when we are already stretched with the war."

Tabitha ignored Bethany Anne's sarcasm. "And I can't blame you for that."

Bethany Anne gave her a very pointed look. "If you're done? I need to keep this short and sweet. I have more meetings than hours today. I'm sending you to the K'nthel system. There's a situation there that requires the delicate touch of a Ranger."

Barnabas snickered. "Delicate? *Tabitha?*"

"Hey, I can be *very* delicate," Tabitha protested.

"You just very delicately fell off a roof again, let's not forget," Hirotoshi reminded her with a small smug smile.

Barnabas paled. "Let's not mention the word 'roof' again for a while. I just had the most unpleasant flashback."

Bethany Anne raised an eyebrow. "A flashback to what?"

Barnabas shook his head. "You don't want to know. Suffice it to say I tripped and fell into the abyss of Tabitha's mind and we will leave it there."

Bethany Anne raised an eyebrow in Tabitha's direction.

Tabitha shrugged. "What?" She made a face at Hirotoshi and searched her memory for any recollection of the name of the star system. "Should I know about this place already?"

Bethany Anne shook her head. "No, I've kept it off the radar deliberately, I have some R&D going on that I want to keep close. The planet I'm sending you to is a spiritual retreat and sanctuary. It's run by a cross between a charitable organization and a religious sect. They call themselves 'the Order of Zaphod.'"

"It's a monastery world?" Tabitha was intrigued. "That's not the kind of place you usually send us."

"Not exactly. The Order is dedicated to helping those in need. I found the system almost by accident, and have been funneling people there who need more care than I can provide at the moment. They fund themselves, for the most part." Bethany Anne sighed. "This war hasn't just been expensive financially, Tabitha. You ever want to know why I hate the Leath so much and not just the Kurtherians they worship? Take a tour of the planet and visit the people who the Order take care of."

Tabitha lowered her eyes. "I can guess what that's like. I'll do whatever I can to help."

Bethany Anne nodded. "I expect nothing less. I have a duty of care to these people, and they are in some kind of trouble."

Tabitha tilted her head. "Oh, yeah? What's the issue?"

Bethany Anne shrugged. "I'm not entirely sure. It's out of the way and communications there are limited, which was one of the reasons I chose it in the first place. I can't go and investigate personally. There's just no way I can leave while we're eyeballs-deep in this fucking war. But I didn't receive the last scheduled update from the Order, and it has me concerned."

"So you want us to go out there and…"

"Find out what's going on, obviously. Make sure that whatever it is hasn't fucked with the Order, and lay down some of my Justice on whoever is responsible for any bullshit you find. Standard Ranger stuff, like I said." Bethany Anne's eyes unfocused for less than a second, and then they were entirely focused—on Tabitha. "I've just sent the information to Achronyx. Make sure you review his report this time. You weren't in the game on Flex."

Tabitha felt her cheeks warm, and she opened her

mouth to protest but was halted by Bethany Anne's raised eyebrow.

"I'm not done. I know you're grieving. Shin's loss hit you harder than anyone else. But you have to find a way to deal with it that doesn't compromise your safety out there." Bethany Anne put a hand over hers. "I'm not angry. I'm worried about you, Tabitha."

"We all are," Barnabas added.

Tabitha looked at Hirotoshi and Ryu for backup, but they just nodded in agreement with Bethany Anne and Barnabas. *Traitors.* She sighed. "I know I was reckless."

Bethany Anne snorted. "There's reckless, and then there's increasing the bounty on your own head for kicks. Running off without your team." The sound of Bethany Anne's nails tapping cut the silence. "Not to mention refusing to use your EI to enhance your chances of success on the mission."

"Damn Achronyx," Tabitha muttered. "The bounty increase wasn't reckless. It was a well-thought-out strategy to rid the planet of its more dangerous assholes and to prevent the chaos of every two-bit punk on the planet coming after me for the quite frankly insulting bounty that was originally put out. Come to think of it, I'm pretty sure I got the idea from you."

Bethany Anne's fingers stopped their tapping. "You are not *me*, Tabitha. You keep throwing yourself in without being prepared, and you're going to get killed, or worse."

Tabitha snickered. "What's worse than getting killed?"

Barnabas caught her attention and indicated Hirotoshi and Ryu. "How about getting one of *them* killed? Tabitha, just take care of yourself, especially since half your team will be unavailable."

Tabitha frowned. "Why?"

Barnabas pressed his lips together. "I need Jun, Katsu, and Kouki for another task."

"We'll manage." Tabitha flashed a grin at Bethany Anne and Barnabas and stood to leave. "I can't promise anything except that I'll get the job done." She grabbed her coat and motioned to Hirotoshi and Ryu to follow. "What if the situation calls for something dramatic?"

Bethany Anne closed her eyes and sighed. "Hire a theater company. You're there to investigate, and then resolve whatever problem you find—*quietly*. Think of it as a lesson in subtlety."

Tabitha didn't see how that was going to work since the drama managed to find her wherever she went, but whatever. "Fiiine."

Bethany Anne called after her as she swept out of the room, Hirotoshi and Ryu close behind, "And read the damn *report*. Achronyx will tell me if you don't."

Bethany Anne turned to Barnabas as the door closed behind Ryu. "Remind me of this moment if I ever think of having children."

QBS *Achronyx*, Bridge

They were about an hour out from their destination. Tabitha was asleep in her captain's chair with her feet up on the console when Achronyx interrupted.

"Ranger Tabitha, my report is ready."

Tabitha opened her eyes and made a face at the speaker

beside her head. "Can it wait? I was getting my beauty sleep."

"Ranger Tabitha, the Empress was very clear about this."

Tabitha yawned and stretched. "Just give me the damn report already. You know I owe you for snitching to Bethany Anne in the first place. I bet you didn't tell her *why* I haven't been reading them when you were telling tales."

Achronyx almost sounded hurt. Almost. "I do not actually know why you refuse to read my reports. I put a lot of effort into them."

Tabitha knew that tone. Whatever Achronyx had planned would be embarrassing, that was a certainty. However, she had resolved to pull her shit together for the mission even before the mini-intervention back on the *Meredith Reynolds*, so she might as well take her medicine without complaining.

She took her feet down and sat up to look at the screen. "Whatever. Let's just get this over and done with so I can finish my nap."

Achronyx brought his report up onscreen. Tabitha tried to swipe past the first page, which contained a video and nothing else. "This is exactly what I'm talking about, snitch." Tabitha winced as she watched herself dangling from the gargoyle and pointed at the screen. "How did you even get this? And what's with the circus music?"

"Just seemed…appropriate," Achronyx replied. "The Empress certainly thought so."

"You showed it to…" Tabitha buried her face in her hands. "You know what snitches get, right?"

"Due rewards and the satisfaction of knowing they did the right thing?"

"Stitches, Achronyx. They get stitches."

"I thought you liked snitches?" Hirotoshi asked from the doorway.

Tabitha spun her chair around. "I like snitches who work for *me*, not ones who run off telling tales to Bethany Anne. You know she's not going to just sit on that video."

Hirotoshi came onto the bridge and took his chair. "Probably not. So what are you going to do?"

Tabitha screwed her face up in thought, then shrugged. "Nothing I *can* do, except give Snitchy McTattletale here his well-deserved stitches. Unless, of course, this video disappears in the next five seconds and he makes it up to me by reading his report out loud." The video was replaced by the real report. Tabitha sat back, put her feet back in their customary position on the console, and closed her eyes. "Good. Now, what are we heading into?"

"You were serious?" Achronyx sounded surprised. "Okay, then. The K'nthel system has one planet that supports life, and two satellite—"

Tabitha waved impatiently. "Yeah, Bethany Anne told us that already. Skip to what I don't know. Who is our contact there?"

Achronyx sniffed. "I'm getting to it, Ranger Tabitha. Two satellite stations around the planet, one of which caters to the tourist industry. It is run by a cooperative, which works in conjunction with the Order of Zaphod to maintain the balance between the spiritual needs of the Order and the expenses associated with the running of the planet's charitable efforts. The other station belongs to the Empress."

"We aren't going there first?"

"No, and probably not at all unless the situation calls for it. First, you must meet with the Order and pick up your permits, then you are to meet with the cooperative."

Tabitha frowned. "They can't just send the permits?"

Achronyx paused. "That is not the way things are done there. Unfortunately, the Order believes that the way to spiritual enlightenment is through a lack of technological reliance."

Tabitha grimaced. "It's not... Please, Achronyx, tell me we're not going to a tech-ban world."

"If I did I would be lying. The laws here state I must not be active. I will be in hibernation from the moment we reach the system, so please do not crash the ship. However, the permits *will* allow you limited access to your personal tech."

"Ugh, *paperwork!*" Tabitha groaned. "Might as well hog-tie me and ask me to walk. How is a hacker supposed to function without tech?"

Hirotoshi smiled. "It will not be all that bad, Kemosabe."

"What do you know?" Tabitha grumped.

He gave her a look of practiced wisdom. "You are talking to a centuries-old vampire, remember? I was alive long before technology took over from the human brain as our primary thought process. What else, Achronyx?"

"After you have obtained your tech permits from the Order, you will head out to the station and meet with the cooperative."

Tabitha interrupted again. "What species make up this Order?"

"The Order is diverse, to represent all sections of the population. It is comprised of a human, a Yollin, a Torcellan, a Skaine—"

"Oh, well, stop right there, Achronyx," Tabitha announced. "We already have our criminal. Case closed. Let's go arrest the scumbag Skaine and get our asses home. No visits to tech-ban planets necessary."

Hirotoshi sighed.

Achronyx chose to let her flippancy go unnoticed. "That is not going to work, Ranger Tabitha. The planetary defenses will take out any ship without the relevant permits."

Tabitha frowned. "So they enforce the tech ban…with tech?"

"Yes," Achronyx confirmed. "Technology provided at the discretion of the Empress, so let's not get me blown up. I like this body."

Tabitha snickered. "Maybe I should refuse. I do owe you a few stitches."

K'nthel System, Planet Zaphod, Temple of Zaphod

Tabitha exited the ship and looked around. They'd landed at the coordinates they had been given on approach —a large open space in a valley just outside the temple complex. The temple had been built at the top of the peak, and smaller buildings dotted the path to the top. Tabitha saw that the other mountains in the area had similar constructions. "What's that one called?" She pointed at an especially ostentatious building which stood out in the distance.

"The Temple of Zaphod," Ryu answered.

"What about that one?"

"The Temple of Zaphod."

"What about— Wait, they're *all* called 'the Temple of Zaphod?'" She waited for Achronyx to answer and then remembered he would be offline while they were in-system. "Hirotoshi?"

Hirotoshi didn't answer. He was gazing around with an expression Tabitha had never seen on his face. "Hirotoshi? You okay?"

He shook himself and dragged his eyes away from the sloping tiered roof of the main temple. "Yes, I am fine. And yes, all of the temples carry the same name."

Tabitha glanced around again. "I wonder who this Zaphod is to get all this?"

"Zaphod is more a state of being than any one entity," a voice cut in from their left.

Tabitha turned to the voice, which belonged to a human in a long, hooded robe. *Ooh, do you think this guy shops at the same place as Barnabas?*

Ryu snickered in her mind.

The monk peered at Tabitha from beneath his cowl. "I assume you are the Empress' Ranger?"

Tabitha nodded and flashed her badge. "Ranger Two. You can call me Ranger Two."

The human spread his hands wide and smiled beatifically. "Welcome to Zaphod, Ranger. I am Brother Cuthbert, and I'll be your guide this blessed day." Cuthbert swept an arm toward the temple. "Shall we?"

Do not say a single word, Kemosabe. Hirotoshi's tone held worry.

Tabitha had no intention of insulting the monk, but there was no fun in telling Mr. Stuffy-pants that. *But his name is Cuthbert! How can I leave that alone? Besides, he looks so spaced out on happy-happy joy-joy vibes that he'd probably laugh along anyway.*

Tabitha was actually a little creeped out by the serenity the monk exuded, but she had promised herself she would suck it up for the mission, so she smiled sweetly. "Of course. Thank you, Brother Cuthbert."

If I did not know you better, I would think you meant that, Hirotoshi told her.

If I didn't know better, I'd think you wanted to join Ryu in his push-ups. I haven't forgotten them, by the way, Ryu.

I hadn't either. It is a shame we won't have an opportunity to play double or nothing here.

Tabitha narrowed her eyes at him and set off to follow Cuthbert up the steps carved into the side of the mountain. *Oh, there's always an opportunity to play. We're just not looking for it at this time.*

Who are you, and what have you done with Tabitha? Ryu demanded straight-faced. *Our Lady Kemosabe would never suggest such a sensible course of action.*

"Bite me," she told Ryu aloud.

Cuthbert turned back in surprise at the sound of her voice.

She waved him on. "Sorry, Brother."

The monk nodded and continued to lead them up the mountain. When they reached the top of the steps, Brother Cuthbert turned away from the wide stone walkway and chose a thin, well-worn path. He saw Tabitha's look and pointed out a small door in the side of the temple. "We will avoid the crowds this way."

He took them into the temple, which was filled with light and color from the stained-glass windows. Those were evenly spaced, with statues representing the deities of many different races.

Tabitha noticed a vaguely human-looking statue. "Who is that supposed to be?" The red eyes gave it away, but she had to ask.

Cuthbert smiled and blushed. "It was made by a visitor from outside the Empire. It is the Empress."

Tabitha snickered. "Well, I suggest you don't let her find out she's being worshipped as a goddess. She hates all the bowing and scraping enough."

Hirotoshi nodded in agreement. "Complete supplication would be a step too far. People should be responsible for their own lives. I would not recommend you encourage this practice."

Cuthbert hastily covered the statue, and they continued into the temple. He answered Ryu's and Hirotoshi's questions about the Order and their history as he led them through the corridors to a room near the heart of the building. Tabitha walked behind and pretended not to listen. The closer they got to the center, the more concentrated the hum of the crowd in the public area grew.

"It's pretty loud out there," Tabitha remarked. "Isn't that kind of the opposite of peaceful contemplation?"

"We work to find a balance between our own needs and the needs of the weary." Cuthbert pushed open the door and indicated they should enter. "The Order will see you now."

Hirotoshi nodded at this. Tabitha shrugged and followed him inside.

"Peace be with you, Brother Cuthbert. Greetings, Ranger."

Tabitha frowned at the oddly unelaborate Torcellan male who stood up to greet them. She only knew he was Torcellan and not just a *really* pale human by his eyes, since his head was shaved clean and he wore a homespun robe similar to Cuthbert's. He stopped talking and left the raised plinth where he was sitting on a table with a four-legged Yollin, an Ixtali, and a...

"Skaine." Tabitha's hand went to her—at the moment useless—JD Special.

"Brother Scroat is among the most enlightened of us all," Cuthbert chided with a pointed look at her waist. "And we do not commit such base acts as violence here."

This Skaine is accepted here. I do not think you should treat him as you usually do, Hirotoshi warned.

He's a fucking Skaine. There is only one type, and I'd be willing to bet he's the source of whatever shady business is going on around here.

Ryu cut in, *I'm not taking that bet.*

Hirotoshi's eyes were on the Skaine. *I accept. He knows you are here, yet he hasn't run. That alone suggests he has done nothing wrong. Reserve your judgment for now. We have a job to do.*

Again, Hirotoshi, he's a Skaine. Of course, *he's done some-*

thing wrong. I just don't know what it is—yet. I'll leave it for now, but when I find out, I'm gonna bring the pain to Brother Skaine.

Scroat appeared to be above such concerns. He had the same serene demeanor as Cuthbert. It was beyond weird to see the caring, slightly absent smile on a Skaine face, but Tabitha wasn't going to be fooled by *that* act.

The Torcellan waved them forward. "Welcome, Ranger. I am Brother Silan, and we are glad to have you here."

Hirotoshi and Ryu followed Tabitha over to the table and placed themselves at her back after she took the seat Silan offered while he introduced the others. *Let's poke the nest a little, see what scurries out.*

You may want to obtain the permits first, Hirotoshi told her. *Leaving the system without them would be difficult.*

No pissing them off before I can shoot my way out. Got it.

Tabitha held the small sphere Silan had given her up to examine it and looked at the assembled monks. She had answered their questions and filled in their paperwork— on actual paper— and now she had the means to circumvent the planet's tech restrictions in her hand. "Interesting. So I just keep this activated and the dampening field is disabled for my weapons and EI?"

A ripple of murmured dismay went through the Order.

Silan shook his head. "Ranger, we apologize, but we were unaware you had brought an artificial entity along with you. Such technology is illegal on this planet."

"How do you get anything done without computers?" Tabitha asked incredulously.

"We have computers," Silan corrected, "but we operate them ourselves."

Tabitha thought that was just make-work, but she wasn't there to judge. Not about their hang-ups, anyway. Discrimination was another matter, though. "And you have no problems with excluding digital beings? They are people too, you know."

Silan frowned as though she'd said something ridiculous. "Of course they aren't people. They are a mockery of life, and as such are not tolerated here."

Tabitha raised an eyebrow but bit back her initial reply. Bethany Anne would hear about this. "Okaaay, then. No EI on-planet; got you. My weapons are good though, right?"

Silan looked around the others, who each did a variation on a shrug. "As long as you can prove you had cause if you use them, there will be no penalty."

By-the-book stinks sometimes. I want you two to know that. She shrugged. "So, what's the problem? My Empress didn't give me much to go on." She gave the monks her most winning smile and noted their reactions.

The Torcellan was genuinely confused. "Why so? We sent a detailed communication in the last window requesting her aid as per our agreement."

Tabitha shook her head. "Um, the Empress didn't receive her scheduled communication, which is why I am here. Why don't you run me through what's been going on?"

Watch our human, Hirotoshi told Tabitha and Ryu.

I see him, Ryu responded.

Cuthbert's slight squirm in his seat told Tabitha plenty. She watched him from the corner of her eye while Silan talked. *I'd be squirmy too if I had to play nice with a Skaine.*

The guy's probably worried he's going to be eaten or something. In fact, look. They're all a little off with him.

"We are not exactly sure." Silan's face was drawn. "Our liaison has reported a strike among the workers. It has us worried. The station is the Order's main source of income, and we rely on that income to carry out our mandate."

Tabitha frowned. "What mandate?"

The Yollin nodded, her mandibles clicking rapidly in her passion. "Our mandate is to provide a haven for anyone in need. We take in the sick, the dispossessed, and the unwanted. We give them a home and a new life."

Tabitha nodded. "It's good work. I knew Bethany Anne had sent people here, but I had no idea of the scale you're operating at. I have to tell you, I'm impressed."

Scroat spoke for the first time. "Yes, Ranger. Zaphod has long been a port in the storm of life. Many find their way here for reasons other than war, and we offer sanctuary to them all. However, this does not come cheaply. We have a whole planet of the needy, the tired, and the broken to tend to. Without the profit the station brings, those people will suffer. You have to resolve this, Ranger. For *them.*"

CHAPTER 3 TABITHA

K'nthel System, Traveler's Rest, Docks

Tabitha strutted down the ramp and headed straight into the crowd. "You guys can deal with all this," she called back with a wave at the ship. "I'm going to find us somewhere good to eat."

By the time Hirotoshi and Ryu caught up with Tabitha, she was on her second plate of something somewhere between nachos and putty, and was still no more comfortable with Scroat's declaration than she had been when they'd left Zaphod. She indicated the plates at the empty spaces, which contained more of the same food. "I ordered for you both. You know, I never get tired of alien food."

Ryu eyed his plate suspiciously as he sat down. "They didn't have any human food?"

Tabitha winked. "Of course they did. Eat up, Ryu."

Hirotoshi gingerly tried a bite. "Hmm. It isn't completely unpalatable once you get past the flavor. And the texture."

"And the way your brain screams at you not to eat it?"

Tabitha shrugged and picked up her glass. "You can't have everything. So I know you kept your eyes open on your way here. What are your impressions? Hirotoshi first. What did you see?"

Hirotoshi picked his glass up and took a sip. "Advertising. Everywhere. This show, this fight, this restaurant. It's never-ending."

Ryu nodded. "This place is all about comfort and entertainment. It's as if they're partying extra hard up here to make up for the simplicity of life on the planet below."

Hirotoshi pointed at Ryu. "Exactly."

Tabitha poked at the remains of her food with a finger. "I didn't get the impression that the Order knows how fast and loose it is here. Or that they would approve, either. I mean, have you ever seen a bald Torcellan before? Those guys are ascetics, for sure. Not one of them checked me out. That takes restraint."

Ryu grinned. "And now we get to the heart of the matter."

Tabitha shrugged. "Not really."

"Scroat?" Hirotoshi asked.

"I just can't work out his game," she confessed. "What is he gaining by pretending to care?"

"Have you considered that the Skaine is not playing any game?" Hirotoshi asked. "I believe we should begin our inquiries a little closer to home."

"Cuthbert?" Tabitha laughed. "He's obviously harmless. I'm telling you the Skaine is our culprit, and I'm going to prove it. Come on, I feel like I can deal with another meeting now that my stomach isn't complaining."

"It might still complain." Ryu snickered. "You keep

eating weird-ass food, and someday your nanos aren't going to save you."

They found the station offices easily. "I miss Achronyx," Tabitha bitched as they approached the reception window. "Don't tell him I said so, though. I don't want his ego getting too big."

The receptionist, a Torcellan, stood up in mild alarm and shut the window when he saw Tabitha and the Tontos coming toward him. Tabitha pulled her badge out on its chain and held it against the glass. "It's okay. We're expected. Tell your bosses that Ranger Two is here."

The receptionist picked up the phone and spoke briefly, then pressed a button to buzz them through to the offices. He eyed them nervously as they walked away.

Tabitha wiggled her fingers at the receptionist as she walked through. "Toodles!"

The meeting room beyond contained a huge window which showed a panoramic view of the planet below. The dozen or so people around the table ceased their hushed argument as soon as the door opened, but Tabitha had already heard the not-so-magic word—trafficking.

She didn't wait for an explanation.

She strode over to the table at vampiric speed, turned the head chair around, and straddled it. "So, what are we trafficking? Do tell. I'm *dying* to know."

Hirotoshi and Ryu glided in and shut the door. The group around the table, mostly humans and Torcellans with a few others sprinkled in, gaped at her sudden appearance. The humans recognized her straight away and fell silent.

Tabitha fixed them all with a hard look. "Well? What is it? Weapons? Drugs? People?"

"You had best tell her," Ryu called from his spot by the door.

"I hope it is not people, for your sakes," Hirotoshi warned.

"Or ours," Ryu added. "It always generates so much paperwork when we have to execute slavers."

Tabitha glanced at the door. "There's paperwork involved?"

"Achronyx does yours," Hirotoshi informed her.

Tabitha tilted her head. "I didn't know that. Anyway," she turned her attention back to the table, "you were about to tell me what it is you're involved with."

The lone Noel-ni at the table bared his teeth at them. "We don't have to tell you humans anything. How did you even get in here?"

Tabitha tapped her badge, which was still hanging loose over her shirt. "You obviously don't understand how this works." She reached into her coat pocket and withdrew the sphere given to her by the Order. It twinkled as she held it up to the light, and the Noel-ni got even angrier.

"Where did you get that?" he demanded. "Only the Order can issue... Oh. You are here about the missing people."

"Nice of you to catch on finally." Tabitha placed the hand holding her JD Special on the table. "Now, if I have your complete attention? *I* am an Empress' Ranger, and *you* are all in a world of shit if you don't start talking."

Tabitha was almost disappointed by the relief that washed over the cooperative. Half of them jumped up and began speaking over each other, and the others leaned in to whisper to each other. Tabitha couldn't keep track, but she knew Hirotoshi and Ryu were paying attention. "Sit *down.*" She flashed red eyes at the Noel-ni from earlier, who was screaming at them all to keep quiet, then pointed at one of the more assertive-looking humans. "*You* be quiet. You, explain why I heard you all talking about trafficking before I decide to arrest every single one of your asses and drag you in front of the Empress."

Her threat had the desired effect. The group all took their seats again, a couple of them still grumbling under their breath at being forced to comply.

The human Tabitha had singled out looked more embarrassed than anything. "We apologize for our lack of hospitality, Ranger." He squirmed uncomfortably in his seat. "I assure you that none of us are involved in any illegal activities. We were merely speculating as to the root of our issue. It is our responsibility to raise income for the Order, one we all take extremely seriously."

Tabitha leaned on the back of the chair. "So all this is approved by the Order?"

He nodded. "Of course. Not all of the weary are in need of tranquility. We deal in most marketable services here. The wealthy pay a premium to access the station's services, and the Order is pragmatic about where their funding comes from."

One of the others, a Torcellan, spoke up. "We pride ourselves on our ability to meet the needs of almost any visitor to the station, which means we allow a certain amount of less family-oriented activity on the upper levels."

Tabitha raised an eyebrow. "What kind of 'activity?'"

"The kind that makes us nervous you are here, Ranger," the Torcellan answered. She was dressed in a flowing semi-diaphanous robe. It was the traditional bland color that Torcellan females wore but was cut to flatter.

Tabitha waved her concern away. "If you mean the fights, I already know about them. What I'm interested in is getting to the bottom of this, so how about you rewind back to when people started going missing?"

The Torcellan shook her head. "The fights are not the main issue, although that revenue stream has also dried up a little recently. The revenue drop is a direct result of the adult entertainment workers' union calling a strike. Of course, the Order doesn't want to hear about the ins and outs of the industry, just that it is regulated and profitable."

The human rubbed his forehead with a hand. "Business has ground to a halt because the union is refusing to lift the strike until the cause of the missing courtesans is determined."

Tabitha nodded. "So you need me to find out what happened to the missing people. Do you have any idea at all what happened to them?"

The Torcellan female nodded. "That was what we were discussing when you...arrived so suddenly. The issue is not confined to the upper levels, Ranger. There have been a few other worker disappearances across the station, and even the odd tourist, but we have been unable to link them to the missing courtesans, and we can find no trace of the missing. Thus we conclude the missing are being stolen and sold into slavery."

"I'm going to need to see everything you have on all of the disappearances." Tabitha wished Achronyx was there to dig through the station's security archives. "Then I want to speak to the workers, as well as anyone else who may have been involved."

"Of course, Ranger," the human replied. "Although I do not think you will find anything of use. The fights are strictly regulated, but as you can imagine we cannot possibly monitor the adult entertainment areas closely." His face was a deep shade of pink as he spoke. "We have to safeguard our better-known patrons' personal comfort."

"Personal comfort—that's a new one." Tabitha holstered her JD Special and stood to leave. "You can make up for your rude reception by giving me what you have, and directions to the admin offices. It's the one thing I haven't seen advertised in this place and I cannot be bothered to hack you."

The elevator opened onto an ordinary, if tastefully decorated, atrium. Hirotoshi and Ryu followed Tabitha to the reception desk next to the elevator, where a human woman greeted them with a smile.

"Hi. I'm afraid we're not taking bookings at the moment." She looked Tabitha up and down appreciatively. "More's the pity."

Tabitha grinned and showed the woman her Ranger ID.

"I'm here to talk about the disappearances," she glanced at the woman's nametag, "Stacy."

Stacy wasn't quite listening. "Mmm-hmm?" She raised an interested eyebrow at Hirotoshi and Ryu, who flanked the elevator. "What are they here for?"

Tabitha snapped her fingers to draw Stacy's attention to her badge. "They are my guards. Focus, Stacy. You can drool over them later. Right now I need to speak to whoever runs things here."

Stacy dragged her eyes away reluctantly. "That would be me."

Tabitha nodded. "Were you listening? I'm here about the disappearances."

Stacy's eyes widened when Tabitha's words finally sunk in. "You are? Oh, at last! I'll go and get the book. Wait here a minute, please."

Tabitha watched Stacy dash through a door behind the desk, presumably into an administration office. She glanced over her shoulder at Hirotoshi and Ryu. *Please tell me I'm not that easily distracted.*

Oh, no, Ryu replied.

That would be lying, Kemosabe, Hirotoshi finished.

I'm standing on both your backs while you do your push-ups, you pair of smart-asses.

I didn't have any push-ups, Hirotoshi pointed out.

The key word there is "didn't." Now you do, and I'm going to stand on your backs just like Bethany Anne would. In fact, I'm going to stand with one foot on each of you, and you can do them in sync until I'm satisfied.

The men groaned. Stacy returned just as they made the noise and glanced at them with a small smirk just touching the corner of her mouth. "They are wasted on guard duty," she told Tabitha. "Here." She passed Tabitha a ledger. "This is the visitor log for the level."

"I'm going to need to take this with me," Tabitha told her.

Stacy nodded. "Okay, since you're a Ranger. But please take care of it. If some of our patrons were aware we even kept this much…let's just say we'd be out of business faster than you can say 'lickety-split.'" Stacy clapped a hand over her mouth when she realized what she'd said. "I'm so sorry!"

Tabitha snorted. "Don't be. You're wasted behind a desk, Stacy."

Stacy twinkled at Tabitha. "I'm happy here, Ranger. Or at least I will be when I know what happened to my friends and colleagues. You're going to find out, right?"

Tabitha nodded. "That's why I'm here. You can help by telling me everything you know." She leafed through the first few pages of the ledger and frowned until she saw the key written out painstakingly on the inside back cover. "Starting with who went missing and when."

Stacy smiled again and motioned for Tabitha to come around the desk to the room beyond. "I was about to take a break. Have you eaten yet? You're welcome to join me."

Tabitha grinned. "It would be rude to refuse." She turned to Hirotoshi and Ryu. "She's right, you guys *are* wasted on guard duty. I'll be fine here with Stacy. Go explore the station and have some fun. Just keep your eyes open for anything suspicious. I'll meet you back on the ship later."

Hirotoshi and Ryu nodded and left. Tabitha made her

way around the desk and followed Stacy into what turned out to be a tidy little office with a couch and a small food preparation area off to one side. Stacy headed over to the fridge and took out a stack of tubs. "Take a seat, Ranger. I hope you don't mind sandwiches?"

"That's great," Tabitha replied. "And you can call me Tabitha."

"I could never, Ranger." Stacy brought two plates over and handed one to Tabitha. They ate as Stacy answered Tabitha's questions.

"I can't tell you how glad I am that you're here," she told Tabitha. "At first when Lucia and Bardoc went missing, we thought they might have eloped. It happens from time to time when people fall in love and decide to start fresh. But then it happened again, and that's when we started to get worried. We all knew the Loren wouldn't leave."

Tabitha tilted her head in question. "I've never seen a Loren. What's so special about them?"

"You would have to meet one to understand. Let's just say tentacles in all the right places and leave it at that. When the Loren vanished, we all got so scared we got together with our rep and demanded she do something. The strike hasn't kept us safe, though. There have been three more disappearances since it went into effect." She bowed her head, her voice quiet. "None of us feels safe. How can we?"

Tabitha sighed. "The Order didn't mention any of this. Neither did the station leaders."

Stacy frowned. "That surprises me. The people down there on the planet rely on the income this station generates." She shrugged. "I don't want to make a big deal out of it, but a big chunk of that is earned by the sex workers. It's a point of pride among the courtesans that we do so much good all around. We need to work to earn a living, but we can't work in fear. It kind of spoils the mood for most, you know?"

Tabitha could imagine. She patted Stacy's hand and stood to leave. "We're going to get to the bottom of this. You can relax, knowing you helped, and I can start building a list of suspects using the ledger. Contact me if you think of anything else, okay?"

Stacy nodded sincerely as she picked up their empty plates. "I will. Thank you, Ranger."

Tabitha tucked the ledger under her arm and took her leave of Stacy. She spent another hour chatting with a few of the courtesans before she made her way back to the ship. The consensus was clear; they were all afraid, and none of them had a clue who was behind the disappearances. This had not turned out to be anything like the assignment she'd imagined when Bethany Anne had sent them out here.

Hirotoshi and Ryu were nowhere to be seen aboard the *Achronyx*. She decided to give them a little longer. "Achronyx," she called as she entered the bridge. There was no reply. "C'mon, quit sulking, Achronyx. I know you're not switched off, I can feel you at the back of my brain." She dropped into her captain's chair and opened the ledger. "I've got a mystery for you."

Well, I suppose they can't find me here.

"Achronyx, are you scared? The dampening field doesn't affect you. You're safe."

Of course not. I do not have the capacity to feel fear.

41

However, my algorithms for self-preservation are working over-time in this place. The absolute opposite of safeguarding my continued existence would be to announce my presence in a system where I am an illegal entity. I examined the defense system the Empress provided. She wants these people safe, and while the planet's field cannot harm me, some of the other features in the network can. I will remain here, thank you, Ranger Tabitha.

Tabitha screwed up her nose. "Yeah, well, it's discrimination, and it sucks. We need to get out of here for a while." She closed the ledger with a clap and opened a mental link to Hirotoshi and Ryu. *Hirotoshi, where are you guys?*

We are currently engaged in competition, Kemosabe. Do you need us?

No. I'm going to leave the system to call Bethany Anne. Will you guys be okay for a few hours or do you want me to wait for you to get back here?

Go ahead. We will be fine, Ryu told her.

Okay. You two play nice, now. She closed the mental link. "Okay, Achronyx, let's get our asses out of here so you can breathe easy and I can call Bethany Anne."

Achronyx came out of hiding the moment they reached the boundary of the defense system. "Thank you. I know this was not strictly necessary."

"Couldn't have you getting cabin fever," Tabitha teased. "We can't stay out here too long, though. I don't want to leave Hirotoshi and Ryu alone on the station any longer than we have to. Open a secure link to Bethany Anne, please."

"Very well," Achronyx acceded.

The Empress was somewhat surprised to see her. "I

wasn't expecting to hear from you just yet. Did you find out what the issue is?"

Tabitha threw her hands up. "Which one?"

Bethany Anne sat forward, instantly concerned. "That bad? Do you need backup?"

Tabitha shook her head. "No, it's nothing the three of us—"

"Four of us. You always forget me," Achronyx complained.

Tabitha would have snarked him into submission, but she was still sore about the treatment he'd received on Zaphod. "Four. Sorry, Achronyx. The *four* of us have got it under control. But Bethany Anne?"

The Empress tilted her head expectantly.

Tabitha let it all out in a rush. "This place is weird as all hell. They enforce their tech ban with the tech you gave them. They don't recognize digital entities as having rights, and they all act freaky. I can't show you proof because my HUD was disabled at the time, but I met all these monks—"

"The Order," Bethany Anne cut in. "Yeah, they do things a little differently there. Was it Silan's tonsure that did it?"

Tabitha nodded wide-eyed. "Understatement much? So they sent your communication as normal, or so they said. Personally, I think the Skaine had something to do with it not getting to you." She shuddered. "I've got to ask—did you check this place out before you gave them the planetary defenses?"

"No, Tabitha, I just had BMW design a defense system for a planet I knew nothing about." Bethany Anne arched an eyebrow. "What do you think?"

"I think you must have sent Bobcat to look the place

over. Only a drunkard would think this setup is nothing to bat an eye at." Tabitha shrugged. "What? You asked. Do you know how the Order pays for all the charitable work they do?"

Bethany Anne waved a hand. "Of course. They have all the entertainments on the station. They pay for everything that way. I liked the idea. Is that not working out?"

"All except the adult entertainment," Tabitha expanded. "The courtesans have been vanishing without a trace. Which, added to your missing communication just screams of people trafficking, and oh *look*, there's a Skaine in the picture."

Bethany Anne pressed her lips together. "It sounds like your deduction is missing a few steps. What makes you think the Skaine is involved?"

Tabitha huffed in exasperation. "Well, it's not going to be the harmless human monk. I'm pretty sure he's too high on good deeds to even think impure thoughts. The Yollin was the same. Nope, my money is on the Skaine."

Bethany Anne pursed her lips. "What bet did you all make?"

"I bet that the Skaine is the bastard doing this. Ryu refused the bet at first, but Hirotoshi took it and went for the human. He's wrong, though. It's definitely the Skaine. There's no such thing as a good Skaine."

Bethany Anne shrugged. "I'm inclined to agree. However, you are operating as an ambassador of the law, and you have to act like one. Do you have any proof the Skaine is involved?"

Tabitha winced. "Well...not yet. But I'll find it, and I'll find out what happened to the missing workers."

Bethany Anne nodded. "I know you will. I also know that you would never take action without proof."

"What do you take me for?" Tabitha leaned in. "And when I'm done, I'm going to have a serious talk with the Order about their prejudices." Tabitha folded her arms. "Poor Achronyx is too traumatized to even sass me."

"That is not true," Achronyx cut in over the speaker. "You just don't deserve my snark today."

"Aw, Achronyx, that's sweet," Tabitha cooed. She put a hand to the side of her mouth and stage-whispered to Bethany Anne, "See, totally out of character. If he were organic, I'd take him to the doctor."

Bethany Anne lifted an eyebrow. "Remember what I said about keeping things quiet, Tabitha. I will speak with the Order about making an exception for our EIs, but otherwise, you need to respect their wishes. You are not actually hurt, are you, Achronyx?"

"No, my Empress," Achronyx answered sheepishly. "I am simply bored."

Bethany Anne nodded. "So suck it up. You're a big EI. Tabitha, see your assignment through within the strictures of local law, then get your ass home."

Tabitha sighed. "You've got it."

CHAPTER 4 TABITHA AND NICKIE

K'nthel System, Traveler's Rest, Entertainment Level, Arena Three

Hirotoshi and Ryu stood back to back in the center of the wide oval and worked a less deadly version of their craft than usual. The crowd bayed as one opponent after another fell at the hands of the ancient Japanese vampires.

The fighters surrounded them but lost the advantage of numbers when they attacked in twos and threes, which made it easier for the Tontos to defend. *Why do they always want to play the big hero? If they all rushed us at once, they'd maybe have a chance.* Ryu punched a Yollin in the mandibles, pulling his fist back on the snap before the Yollin bit down. *Surely they know they can't win this way. We've been fighting for over an hour now. It's obvious we're not going to tire.*

Hirotoshi's eyes sparkled as he spun and kicked the unknown alien in front of him, then followed through with an elbow to the face of the one who replaced it. *This is the best workout we've had in a while.*

At least since we broke up that Skaine slave meet, Ryu agreed. *I'm getting bored with this. Want to do the wall of death?*

Only if you promise to never tell Tabitha we cut loose like this. I have a reputation to uphold. Hirotoshi chuckled. The fighters appeared to have realized their lone-wolf tactics weren't working. *They are closing in a little. You may do the honors.* They rotated a few steps and linked arms, then Hirotoshi lifted Ryu and spun him in a fast circle. Ryu stamped and kicked his way around the fighters, sending them flying like bowling pins.

Hirotoshi released Ryu, and they closed in to protect each other once again. The only way to get backstage was to fight and win, and newcomers were expected to lose quickly. The fight boss had seen the potential and thrown everything he had at the Tontos. Consequently, they were surrounded by thirty fighters of varying disciplines and species.

These odds aren't exactly fair, Ryu bitched. *Only thirty? Where's the challenge?*

The challenge here is not to kill anyone. Hirotoshi punted the oncoming Yollin into the crowd. He knocked down a pair of burly humans, who promptly dragged the Yollin to his feet and began laying into him.

True. Shall we end this? Tabitha will be returning soon.

Hirotoshi agreed, and they stepped up their speed to vampiric levels. The fighters dropped like flies around them faster than the crowd could see. The crowd began to howl and throw their trash into the ring, skating the edge of uproar.

The referee decided enough was enough and signaled

the end of the fight. Of course, there was no way a tinny whistle could be heard above the melee. The klaxon to end all klaxons blared, dropping everyone present to their knees with the ear-splitting noise.

The fight boss nodded to Hirotoshi and Ryu and waved them over, then handed them an envelope each and patted them on the back. "Great fight. I'd love to talk to you both about becoming regulars here. You know Harry will take good care of you."

Hirotoshi didn't break the human's hand since that would have been rude and they needed him for the moment. However, if Harry kept referring to himself in the third person, Hirotoshi wasn't sure he would remain so restrained. "We might consider such an offer if the circumstances were right. Is there somewhere we can clean up before we speak?"

The boss summoned a young man. "Take these gentlemen to the VIP changing area. Bring them anything they ask for."

The kid inclined his head and led Hirotoshi and Ryu through the maze of brightly-lit corridors in the backstage area to a sumptuous suite. "There are robes to wear while your clothing is in the autocleaner," he told them enthusiastically. "And the bar is stocked with human-friendly food and drinks." He dipped his head and left them to get settled.

Hirotoshi waited until the door had closed behind their escort to glance at Ryu, whose head was buried in the fridge.

"Human food," Ryu announced. "Is this…" He dumped a

wrinkled cucumber on the side. "And this." He pulled out a small tub and opened the lid to sniff the contents. A pungent sourness filled the air.

"If that is yogurt, I do not want to know which animal they procured the milk to make it from," Hirotoshi stated.

"There are some crackers. Actually, I've changed my mind about being hungry." Ryu sealed the pot and shoved it to the back of the fridge. "I wonder how long Tabitha will be."

"Long enough for us to investigate behind the scenes here." Hirotoshi headed for the door. "I cannot hear anyone outside. Let's go search Harry's office. Something about him did not sit right with me."

They made their way along the corridor, looking into each room they passed. When they reached the junction in the corridor, they chose the opposite direction from the one they'd been brought along earlier. It led them past a series of storerooms, most of which were locked, and eventually ended at a large door.

Hirotoshi took point. He opened the door and slipped inside while Ryu kept an eye on the corridor.

It is clear, Hirotoshi announced a moment later.

They padded silently through the reception area and made short work of the lock on Harry's inner office. Hirotoshi made his way straight to the row of filing cabinets that lined one side of the office.

Ryu opened a desk drawer and began to rummage through the contents. *This is a little like the old days,* he remarked. *You know, before we had ADAM or Achronyx to do all the legwork for us.*

It is certainly nostalgic. Hirotoshi got to work searching the filing cabinets. He flicked through the drawers one at a time, pulling a folder out every now and again to get a closer look at the contents. He came across a section of unmarked files in the middle of a drawer which was at odds with the careful labeling of the others he'd examined. *Ryu, I have found something.*

Already? What have you got? Ryu left the drawer he was searching and came over to the desk.

Hirotoshi handed Ryu the file. *I am unsure at the moment. However, this information is at odds with the rest of the accounting data I discovered. It looks as though Harry has been taking bribes.*

Ryu leafed through the paperwork. *Not just Harry. There are a lot of hints about other people's involvement here. This assignment is getting more complicated. What have we stumbled into?*

Hirotoshi was quiet for a beat while he searched for any other unlabeled files. *It seems that our initial impression of a society working together for the good of all was just that, an impression. I am certain the Empress will be happy to know we are here to take the matter in hand.* He sighed and removed the documents from each file before putting the empty folders back. *I suppose we should be grateful that Harry is the arrogant type.* He sighed and showed Ryu another sheaf of papers.

Ryu peered at the document and shook his head in disbelief. *He's skimming from the profits as well? No wonder they don't argue the no EI rule. This kind of fraud would be discovered in less than a minute. How do they sleep at night?*

See this? It gets worse. This goes beyond financial skullduggery. Hirotoshi handed Ryu the memo he'd just found tacked onto a financial breakdown.

Ryu's eyes widened as he read. He pointed out a name printed on the bottom of one of the documents. *That is one of the leaders—the human who remained silent at the meeting, I believe. Tabitha is not going to take this well.*

You have been working on your gift for understatement, I see. Hirotoshi grimaced. *I am not sure if Kemosabe will be able to restrain herself when she finds out about this.*

Finds out about what? Tabitha's voice cut in. *We're back. You can meet me at the dock and tell me everything.*

On our way, Hirotoshi replied. He hesitated for a moment, then gathered the papers up.

Tabitha made her way to the exit ramp. *I'll be back soon,* she told Achronyx.

I will be here hiding. His voice was small in her mind. *I may decide that this tech-ban world is not so bad if you continue to be so nice to me.*

Don't push it, she teased. *You're still a pain in my ass.*

Hirotoshi and Ryu were waiting when the ramp dropped. They strode up the ramp and past Tabitha.

"What gives?" she asked, perplexed.

We should discuss this somewhere we cannot be seen, Hirotoshi stated.

Ryu nodded. *You're not going to like what we found one bit.*

Tabitha took in the deadly serious looks on both of

their faces as she followed them aboard. "What? What have you found?"

Hirotoshi handed the thick stack of paperwork to her.

She scanned quickly through the documents, discarding each page as she finished it. The line between her eyes deepened with every sheet of paper she dropped, and she finally looked up with reddening eyes. "This will not stand. I will not *allow* it to stand."

Hirotoshi nodded. "I did not expect any less, Kemosabe."

Tabitha looked up at them, the last piece of paper scrunched in her hand, forgotten. "We're going to turn this nest of snakes over and follow the trail of corruption right back to the source."

"And when we find it?" Ryu asked.

Tabitha's face was as hard as stone. "We're going to cut its head off."

Rebus Quadrant, Themis Colony, Aboard the *Penitent Granddaughter*

Nickie emerged from the ship in search of breakfast. Her days of eating cold food from a can were well and truly over. She'd been spoiled by Grim's cooking.

The problem was that Grim hardly bothered to cook aboard the *Granddaughter* anymore, since his culinary skills were much more appreciated by the colonists who attended the communal meals. She had no choice but to join them if she wanted a decent meal.

She entered the mess hall and wove through the diners

until she reached the serving line and found her epicurean Yollin. She grabbed a tray and joined the line. "What's for breakfast, Grimmie-baby?"

Grim's entire body twitched in distaste. "Same as it was yesterday, doll face. Now get your eggs and stop holding up the line."

Nickie narrowed her eyes in mock-rage. "Touché. You win this round." She grinned and held out the tray and Grim dumped her food onto it with a wink. "We're working on the irrigation system today, right?"

Grim nodded. "Durq is already out at the dome. I saw him just after dawn. He said something about Lisa having the afternoon shift and wanting to work in silence."

"Whatever. As long as he does his share." Nickie half-shrugged and took her tray over to a table that had just been vacated. She had barely taken a mouthful when a shadow fell across her. She looked up with a scowl. "What?"

Raynard took an involuntary step back. "I was just going to ask if you wanted some company. I can see you don't, so I'll go." He turned to leave.

Nickie waited for Meredith's rebuke, but it didn't come. She sighed. "Just fucking sit down already." She caught sight of Adelaide hovering behind Raynard. "You too, Adelaide."

Adelaide gave Raynard a little shove with her hip and slipped onto the bench next to Nickie. "I wanted to talk to you about today's tasks. I'm hoping that today is the day we get the water running. To the dome, at least."

Nickie wasn't so sure. "I thought you still had a long way to go with the water line?"

Raynard smiled and patted Adelaide's arm. "Addie and the others have made great progress."

Adelaide nodded in agreement. "We're almost there. It's the last stretch before the colony. The buildings in that area were destroyed completely in the Skaine attack. We have to clear out the rubble and dig down to get to the pipeline before we can even *think* about repairing or replacing it." Adelaide shrugged. "But I'm not going to let a little thing like that get in the way. We have the equipment to get it done, and you have an onboard EI who can interface with it..."

Nickie frowned. "If she will. She's quiet this morning."

Of course, I will, Meredith interjected.

Oh, so you didn't decide to deactivate yourself. I was beginning to wonder.

I was giving you some space, Nickie. You might show a little gratitude.

Someone woke up on the wrong side of the amygdala this morning.

"Nickie?" Adelaide was waving a hand in front of Nickie's face.

Nickie snapped back to reality. "Meredith and I will operate the equipment. Let's get this bitch dug."

Raynard laughed. "You know, that reminds me of what Pete would have said in this situation."

Adelaide giggled. "Oh, you're right!"

He and Adelaide put their heads together and chorused.

"If it ain't a bitch to get it, then it ain't worth it."

"Who the hell wants an easy life?"

A woman from the next table turned around. "What

about 'life's a bastard, then you die?' That was always my favorite."

"Yeah, that one too, Sue." Raynard pushed his food around with his fork. "I always appreciated his outlook; it made the morning interesting. Things are a little different around here without Pete's unique take on things."

"You mean without his constant grousing," Sue retorted.

That raised a laugh, albeit a small one.

The conversation turned back to the day ahead, then Raynard and Adelaide left to get started. Nickie headed back to the breakfast line to see if there was any chance of seconds. Grim joined her shortly after with his own breakfast once everyone had been served. He sat across from Nickie and began to eat. "Did you get your 'things' taken care of last night?"

Nickie looked up from her food, frowning for a moment until she remembered that she'd left dinner early last night. "Oh, yeah. It wasn't a big deal. Something fucking hilarious happened after I left, though. I got a message."

Grim lowered his fork, intrigued. "A message? From who?"

Nickie pointed at him. "That's what *I* wanted to know. And when I found out, I wished I hadn't bothered to open the damn thing at all. I thought we were pretty much hidden out here, but somehow the Federation knew where to find me."

"The Federation?" Grim asked.

Nickie nodded. "I know, right? I couldn't believe it either. I'm sure Meredith had something to do with it, but she's not her usual chatty self today. I suppose there's a first time for everything."

Grim dismissed her grumbling. "Are you going to tell me what the message said?"

Nickie laughed. "That's the best bit! The sender is some royal asshole who wants me to rescue their son. Apparently Prince Precious has gotten himself lost on some idiotic fucking quest and they want me to find him and bring him home."

Grim was silent for a moment. "Shouldn't we look into it?"

Nickie snorted. "Nope. Why would you even suggest it? Let the Federation deal with their own shit. It's not my problem."

Grim's concern was evident. "But if the kid is in trouble... And I don't want you to take this the wrong way, but if his family is contacting you to ask for help, they must be pretty short on hope."

Nickie glared across the table at Grim. "How *else* am I supposed to take it?"

Grim met her stare with a searching look. "Take it that no one else *can* help, Nickie. I know it isn't a ship full of the Skaines you want, or in fact any Skaine, but there is a life in danger. A life that might be in your power to save."

Nickie looked away. "You can save your guilt trip. If I wanted to deal with that shit, I could have stayed home." She pushed her tray away and stood up abruptly. "You know what, I've got better things to do than listen to this." She stalked out of the mess hall and headed to the dome, where the efforts to create a sustainable agricultural biome to offset the inhospitable climate of the colony were coming to a head.

Meredith broke her silence at last. *You know that Grim is right.*

If that's all you're going to say, then you can just go back to ignoring me until I need you to operate the equipment.

Nickie—

Same as I told Grim, save it. We have work to do, work for people who haven't gotten themselves into a shitty situation because they got lost on fucking vacation. She all but stormed over to the site near the dome.

Adelaide waved Nickie over when she saw her approaching. "You're here!" She took a tablet out of her pocket and came to meet Nickie halfway. "I wasn't sure if you were going to make it today after all."

Nickie bit back her snarky reply. It wasn't Adelaide's fault she was in a pissy mood, and she didn't want to make the younger woman cry. "I'm here, and ready to go. What do you need me to do?"

Adelaide looked at her. "The heavy equipment is in that storage shed over there, and the excavator is right at the back. Have you operated this kind of machinery before?" Nickie murmured noncommittally, and Adelaide took that as an affirmative. "Just do your best and Meredith can work the rest out, right?"

Nickie shrugged. "Probably. Where do you need me to dig?"

Adelaide pointed to a marked quadrant in the larger rubble-strewn area. "That's all got to be cleared, then we can begin to gauge the extent of the damage to the pipes beneath and choose our next steps."

Nickie nodded. "Fair enough." She made her way to the shed, which she would have described as more of a warehouse, and wandered through the bays until she found the excavator she was looking for.

She climbed into the cab and jiggled the controls. "Meredith, switch this thing on. Time to get to work."

CHAPTER 5 NICKIE

The morning crawled by. Nickie got to grips with the excavator fairly easily and had cleared the rubble by the time Grim, Melissa, and Keen arrived with lunch sent from the meal hall. She didn't talk to Grim, but then he managed to communicate just fine with a series of increasingly worried glances until she snapped and took her food back to the *Granddaughter*.

She found herself making the turn to her training room, the empty cargo hold she'd claimed. She made the repairs to her punching bag between hurried mouthfuls of food, then re-hung the bag from the girder. When she was done, she stripped down to her tank top and shorts and wrapped her hands.

"Why do I even bother with this?" she muttered as she tore the roll loose from her knuckles and tossed it to the side. "It's not like they won't heal."

Why do you do it, then? Meredith piped up.

Nickie took a stance and began her warm-up, moving slowly and striking precisely. *I don't know.* She stepped up her pace a little. *It's just how I was taught, I guess. That's why it's called training.* She pummeled the bag in silence for a while, losing herself in thought while her body worked through the sets she knew with every fiber of muscle. Grim and Meredith were right. She couldn't ignore a request for help, no matter what the source.

And she couldn't ignore the source, no matter how urgent the request.

Even if it was the most ridiculous fucking situation she'd ever heard of.

Mere?

Yes, Nickie?

I don't know what to do about the lost prince, and I don't like it.

How so?

It's just so fucking complicated! And I hate complicated. Nickie gathered her thoughts while she moved through a tricky combo. *I want to go rescue the dumbass, I really do. Even dumbasses deserve to live. But...the Federation is involved, which of course means my family will have their noses in there somewhere. Why now? Why reject me all this time and then, out of the blue, reveal that they know where I am?*

It is almost time for you to return, Nickie. Two years will pass before you know it, and then you can go home again. Don't you want that?

Nickie wiped the sweat out of her eyes and went at the bag even faster. Her hands were a blur, and her tank top stuck to her as the sweat ran freely down her back. *What if I don't want to go back? What if I've built a new life out here by then? This could be my home, Meredith. It's not so bad, and at least if I decide to care about someone out here, there's nobody who can send them away from me. Why should I go back just so they can take it all away again?*

Do you still feel that way?

Nickie grabbed her towel and wiped her face. *How can I feel anything else? I hate him, and I hate the Federation. If it weren't for them, my Aunt Tabitha would be here with me now. I know it.*

Meredith was silent for a moment. *I cannot agree. I know your family loves you, and that they want what's best for you. Even if it doesn't seem that way right now.*

Families don't abandon members just because they don't like their attitude, and I don't fucking care if you agree. It still doesn't solve my dilemma.

Only you can make that choice, Nickie.

So helpful, Meredith.

Rebus Quadrant, Themis Colony, Agricultural Dome

Grim walked along the half-planted rows looking for Durq. The little Skaine had not appeared at lunchtime, and Grim had not been able to locate him at their living quarters. He hadn't been aboard the ship when Grim checked there either.

He had heard Nickie grunting and growling. She hadn't noticed him when he'd popped his head into the cargo hold she'd commandeered. Clearly, she had been too wrapped up in taking her frustration out on the punching bag.

Grim spotted Durq kneeling between two trellises with his hands buried in the earth and made his way over. "Hey, Durq."

Durq jumped clear off the ground at the sudden sound. "Oh, it's just you, Grim. You scared me."

"Sorry, my mind is on Nickie."

Durq stood and took off his work gloves. "Is she okay? I've stayed out of her way since she got that message. I know she won't hurt me, but she's terrifying when she's emotional."

Grim shrugged. "She's…working through things, I think. All we can do is be there for her while she's vulnerable."

Durq's eyes widened. "Don't let her hear you call her vulnerable. I don't think you'd survive her efforts to prove otherwise." His stomach growled loudly, and he looked hopefully at the container Grim held.

Grim gave it to Durq. "Here, I brought you something to eat. You missed the meal."

Durq accepted gratefully. "Thanks. So do all Yollins do that human shrugging thing now?"

Grim chuckled. "Probably? It's the most useful gesture. How's the planting coming?"

Durq bobbed excitedly. "Really well. As soon as the water restrictions are lifted food production is going to go through the roof." He looked at the overhead sprinklers. "Especially now that construction on the other biomes is nearing completion."

Just then the power cut out and the emergency lighting came on. Grim looked at Durq, expecting the little Skaine to need reassurance.

"It's the third time the power has gone out in as many days. I'm not scared." Durq lifted a shoulder. "Oh, it *is* useful. Would you look at that."

Grim snickered at the surprised look on Durq's features. "Humans—they surprise you every time."

Adelaide swept into the dome like a tiny hurricane holding a toolbox. "Hey, Grim! I hoped that was you I heard. Come with me. I need your back."

Grim and Durq exchanged puzzled glances.

Adelaide waved impatiently. "Come *on!*" She turned on her heel and marched out.

Grim shrugged at Durq and turned to follow her.

"When you said you needed my back, I didn't think you meant like this." Grim squirmed uncomfortably as Adelaide's heel dug into his shoulder. He braced his back against the wall and did his best to keep still.

Her voice echoed slightly in the wall cavity. "Well, I couldn't reach, and I didn't have time to go and find a ladder." She dropped her wrench into his outstretched hand. "These systems don't fix themselves, you know. Pass me the soldering kit."

Grim did as he was told, and after a few more minutes of Adelaide dancing a jig on his shoulders, she passed her tools to him and climbed down from the access panel.

"All done," she told him brightly.

Grim massaged his shoulders. "You've really come to grips with all this. It hasn't been easy, but you and the others have pulled off a miracle in the last few weeks."

Adelaide blushed. "I don't know about that. I always liked fixing things, and there's no shortage of those around here. Besides, it's a lot easier now we're not so focused on outside threats. You and Nickie have made such a difference here." She smiled at Grim and gathered her toolkit. "Come on, there are three more of these, and you make better conversation than any ladder I ever stood on."

Grim chuckled and trailed behind Adelaide from one junction box to another around the colony. All in all, Grim had a pleasant time of it, being used to reach the high places notwithstanding. Adelaide was as sharp as a box of knives and twice as witty, which made for fun all around.

The end of the workday was approaching, but Adelaide showed no sign of stopping. Grim stood off to the side, shining a flashlight for her to work by. Raynard wandered into the storage area they were working in and stood watching in silence with his arms folded.

Grim spotted Raynard and waved him over. Adelaide was bent at the waist inside the junction box and was mostly oblivious to her surroundings. Her foot lifted as she reached farther inside, and a shower of sparks arced out on either side of her.

"What's she doing?" Raynard asked Grim.

"Hell if I know," Grim replied. "Something to get the power back on." He held the flashlight out to Raynard. "Can you take over? I need to get to the mess hall. Dinner won't cook itself."

Raynard nodded. "Sure."

Adelaide popped her head out. She smiled sweetly at Raynard and tilted her head at Grim. "Are you going, Grim? Save us some dinner, yeah? We might be a while."

Raynard visibly deflated.

Grim chuckled. "I'll have something sent over for you

both if you're not back by the end of the first sitting." He waved and left.

Raynard peered into the junction box and wrinkled his nose. "How long do you think this is going to take?"

Adelaide shrugged and bent back over to continue working. "Perhaps a couple hours. Maybe a little more. Why?"

Raynard's eyes were distant. "I have some council business to attend to this evening."

Adelaide looked up. "But we had plans. Did you forget?"

Raynard shook his head. "I didn't, but this has to come first. Maybe we can catch up after that?"

Adelaide held out her hand for the flashlight. "Then go, see to your business. I'll see you later if there's time."

He kissed her cheek distractedly and left. Adelaide watched him go, wondering if she shouldn't feel a bit more put out by Raynard's apparent coolness toward her. She was a little disappointed, but that was all.

Rebus Quadrant, Themis Colony, Control Room

Keen twitched at the squeaking sound his chair made when he rolled from one side of the room to the other to switch his attention from the colony security feeds to the data coming in from the long-range sensors. The noise cut the silence like nails down a chalkboard, momentarily shattering Keen's peace and quiet.

The sensor data showed nothing out of the ordinary. He should enjoy the time freed up by Raynard's recent push to be someone the colony could rely on to get things done. Some would have felt slighted, but not Keen.

He was grateful the younger man had the energy, the kind of energy Keen had felt wane in himself over the last weeks. He'd begun to see things differently since the Skaines attacked the colony. His drive to keep everyone alive and get them free had gotten him through the hardest times, but losing people he knew and cared about, people he was responsible for... It had altered him irrevocably.

Satisfied with the readouts, he scooted back to the center and picked up his tablet. He cursed softly when he saw the clock and realized that the mess hall would be closed now. He rummaged around in the desk in the vain hope of discovering a stray protein bar but was out of luck. He grabbed his tablet instead and opened the e-reader to where he'd left off in his book.

More than a few asked why he stuck by his e-reader when immersive holo-entertainments were easily accessible. Although there were certain...*upsides* to having the scenes played directly into his mind, Keen preferred to use his imagination and make his own interpretation of the world he was stepping into.

There was no escape for him tonight, though. He read without reading, the words just sliding off his brain. His thoughts were too loud for him to enjoy the adventures of the feisty heroine he usually enjoyed so much. It seemed flat, almost contrived. He closed the screen and put the tablet down. He just couldn't lose himself in the story tonight.

There was a soft knock at the door, and Adelaide came in with a covered tray. "Hey, Grim said you missed dinner, so I brought you some leftovers."

Keen smiled. Adelaide was becoming like a daughter

to him; she certainly played the part. "Thank you, Addie." He took note of her slightly strained expression. "What's up?"

Adelaide sighed. "It's nothing much, just... I don't even know how to begin to explain."

Keen furrowed his bushy eyebrows. "A little bit of everything? You look like you have the weight of the world on your shoulders."

Adelaide laughed. "Pots and kettles. You've been hiding in here an awful lot recently."

Keen chuckled. "I'll have you know I've been taking it easy." He waved his tablet at her for emphasis. "Raynard has done a great job of stepping up, and it's left me time for other things. I thought I'd spend it making a difference, but it doesn't seem like there's a lot an old man like me can offer."

Adelaide slapped his shoulder lightly. "Don't you dare say that! You make a hell of a difference, Keen. You held this place together during the worst time we've ever been through. We wouldn't even be *alive* if it wasn't for you. Give yourself a little credit, and admit that you're having trouble adjusting now that we're not fighting just to stay alive." She folded her arms and tapped her foot.

Keen sat back and considered Adelaide's assessment. "Maybe," he admitted eventually. "Maybe I miss the urgency, if not the danger to everyone's lives. Don't get me wrong, I'm glad we can rebuild and move on. But...I don't know. I'm missing something." He shrugged. "It's starting to feel small here, I guess."

Adelaide clapped and pointed at Keen. "Yes! Exactly that. The colony is running almost without issues, and every day there's less for me to do. That's why I was able to get the water issue solved so quickly."

Keen looked up from his food. "Oh, yeah? It's complete?"

Adelaide nodded. "We finished late this afternoon. Nickie and Meredith saved us a bunch of time."

"So what's next?"

Adelaide shrugged. "I don't know. The defenses are built, and the agricultural biomes are pretty much complete. Now that the water is running, I haven't got anything major to test myself against. I want to keep pushing myself, but I can't see how to do that. It's hard to admit, but I think we both have itchy feet."

Keen grinned. "Something like that. I can't deny a desire to get out there again. Open space has a siren song all her own, Addie, and she's singing louder to me with each passing day."

Adelaide's eyes shone. "There's adventure out there. It's just waiting to be discovered. I can't deny that I want to chase it, too. We nearly *died*! I had no hope, Keen. None at all. Then Nickie came along and saved us."

Keen sighed. "That kind of event changes your perspective on things and makes you want to use the time you might not have had to its full potential."

"I've been thinking about it a lot since then," she confessed. "You want to make a difference? Well, so do I. I have more to give than this. I want a change."

Keen hadn't expected such an outburst from the normally collected young woman. "How has Raynard taken this? Have you two talked about it?"

Adelaide shook her head. "No, he's buried in his work,

and honestly, we're not really talking much about anything at the moment. I can't see him being too happy, though. He's so focused on the day-to-day of the colony that there isn't time for us now, or at least it seems that way."

Keen nodded. "We all have to work through what happened. That wasn't a walk in the park we went through, Addie. Raynard's way of coping is to throw himself into work."

Adelaide pressed her lips together. "I suppose I need to work out whether I want to run because it's my reaction, or because I really want to leave Themis."

They were interrupted by Nickie making her typical grand entrance. "Hey, what are you guys doing in here? Don't you know there's a party going on? Quit moping, we're *celebrating*!"

Keen gaped, shocked by the change in Nickie. "Celebrating?"

Nickie grinned. "The water? Melissa and Raynard broke out the good stuff," she paused, "if you can call it good. It's strong, I'll give them that."

Adelaide laughed. This was a whole new side to Nickie, one she'd suspected existed but hadn't expected to see. "Come on, Keen! Everyone is waiting."

Keen shook his head. "I'm good, thanks. You ladies have fun, though."

Adelaide hugged him. "You know we will. I'll make sure to have a drink or three for you."

"Make sure you do," he told her fondly.

She linked her arm through Nickie's and steered her back toward the door. "What are we waiting for? Lead the way."

CHAPTER 6 TABITHA

K'nthel System, Traveler's Rest, Aboard the *Achronyx*

Tabitha and Ryu poured over the paperwork Hirotoshi had taken from the office while Hirotoshi combed through the ledger Stacy had provided.

"I don't get it. Why can't I find anything that points to that damned Skaine?" Tabitha huffed in exasperation. "Are you sure you got all the files, Hirotoshi?"

Hirotoshi gave her a look that would melt stone.

"Okay, okay. This is plenty to start with." She waved the paper at him. "There's enough here to arrest half the officials on the station, just nothing on Brother Scroat. I *know* he's involved in this somehow. Otherwise, how did the Order's plea for help just vanish like that?"

"There are any number of reasons it could have happened," Hirotoshi told her. He looked up from the ledger. "You are allowing your preconceptions to get in the way of the investigation."

"Am not." Tabitha pouted. "What is this? "What's with this sudden denial of the way the universe works? He's a

73

Skaine, and we have missing people. It's not rocket science."

Ryu raised an eyebrow. "Are you so certain that Scroat is involved? I have to agree with Hirotoshi. All the evidence points to this station, and apart from the missing report, there's nothing to connect any of what we've discovered to the Order. Unless you know something we don't?"

"No… But I'm right." She threw her hands up in frustration. "How can you be so sure he's not involved?"

Hirotoshi shrugged. "I am not. However, I am not so quick to assume that Scroat is involved simply because he is a Skaine. Especially since none of the evidence so far points to him."

Tabitha narrowed her eyes. "Yet. It doesn't point to him *yet*. You're going to eat your words when we figure this all out and he's at the center of it. Just wait and see."

Hirotoshi inclined his head a fraction. "And if that is the case, I will accept that I was wrong and move on, having learned a valuable lesson."

"Yeah, we might not be moving on for a while." Tabitha was getting grumpier by the minute. "There's so much corruption going on here, I have to wonder how the Order was getting any funding at all." She discarded the file and picked up the next report. "Old Harry has dirt on people's dirt. I can almost admire him. Oh." She stopped to read the top sheet again. "Guys, this doesn't add up at all."

Ryu held out a hand for the paper. "What is it?"

Tabitha tore the top sheet free and handed it over. "There's a single massive payment here. It disappears almost the moment it hits this first account, and then it looks like it bounces from account to account until... Oh, that's all there is. Hey, this looks like an investigation. Who is behind all these cutouts?" She flipped through the pages of the report slowly. "There's nothing here to say who any of this belongs to, or why Harry was investigating in the first place."

Hirotoshi looked up. "I am having better luck here. I have identified several potential suspects already. Perhaps there is some crossover between the two sets of miscreants?" He flicked to the back of the ledger. "There is rather a lot of detail in here. It appears to be more of a service guide for the wealthier patrons than anything else. Oh joy, there are photos included." His face froze for a second. "Oh. Oh, no."

Ryu got up to look at the photo. "But he's human! Human bodies can't do...*that*."

Tabitha dropped the report onto her chair and came over to see what had shaken the usually unflappable duo. "Show me."

"Are you sure? You will not be able to unsee it afterward." Hirotoshi held the ledger up when she nodded.

Tabitha tilted her head from side to side as her brain tried to make sense of the scene in the photo. "That's just..." She swallowed hard as a lump rose in her throat. "Wow."

"To each their own," Hirotoshi offered diplomatically.

Tabitha rubbed her eyes as if that could remove the image that was now burned into her retinas for at least an eternity. Maybe longer. "Yeah, but that alien seemed *way* too into everyone else's."

Ryu sat down heavily, looking a bit green. "Where did all the tentacles come from?"

Hirotoshi shook his head. "The question is, where did they all go? It is not a question I would like to be answered, however." He turned the page and grimaced. "Humanity amazes me in its capacity to reach for the extreme. This is one of the times I would rather not have witnessed it."

Tabitha had to agree. "I'm not sure I want to brag about being the same species as that guy, that's for sure." She shuddered and went back to her chair to continue her investigation. "Mystery accounts aside, this is all too neat. Like, super-organized. I think Harry is running an extortion racket in addition to his skimming."

Hirotoshi's lip curled in distaste. "What's a little blackmail when you are already stealing from the destitute? Men like Harry are a blight upon humanity. It was only because we have been instructed to keep a low profile that I allowed him to continue breathing. The man made my skin crawl."

"He won't be breathing for much longer if he doesn't change his ways. Tabitha waited for Hirotoshi to finish scanning the last page. "Is there anything about him in the ledger?"

"No," he replied. "This man is too sharp to allow any of his victims to gain an advantage. You can be sure that whatever his proclivities are, no one on this station will have a clue about them."

Ryu nodded in agreement. "He's slick, but he has grown comfortable, and is overly flashy. That makes him vulnerable, which makes him ripe for the turning."

Tabitha grinned. "You want to go and dangle him off a

building by his ankles until he squeals like the little piggy he is?"

"We are on a space station, Kemosabe," Hirotoshi reminded her.

Tabitha rolled her eyes. "Do you have to take everything so literally? An airlock will do the same job. As long as he talks, who cares? But we'll have to find him first. Everyone get some rest. We'll track him down first thing tomorrow."

They were interrupted by a proximity sensor alert.

"Who's out there?" Tabitha jabbed a couple of buttons on the arm of her chair to bring up the ship's external cameras. A human woman danced from foot-to-foot, looking up at the door of the *Achronyx*. "Hang on, she's talking." Tabitha flicked on the audio feed.

"It's Stacy! You have to help, please!"

The woman sat in the chair opposite Tabitha, cradling the hot drink Ryu had made her to help with her shock.

"What's your name?" Tabitha asked. "And what were you saying about Stacy?"

"My name is Safaia," she began. She sipped her tea and put the mug down quickly. "But Ranger, we haven't got time for this. They took Stacy!"

Tabitha sat forward. "*Who* took Stacy?"

Safaia shook her head miserably. "I don't know who they were. I've never seen them before." Her breathing quickened again, and she began to cry.

Tabitha placed a comforting hand on Safaia's wrist. "It's okay. Tell me everything, from start to finish."

Safaia sniffed and wiped her face with her sleeve. "Okay. I was meeting Stacy for drinks after I'd finished work at my day job, I'm a game designer as well as a courtesan, and I've been working extra hard there to make up for the income I've lost out on while the strike is in effect." She sniffed. "So I hadn't seen Stacy for a while. I got up to her office just as they were dragging her out, and all I could do was hide before they saw me too."

Tabitha produced a box of tissues and offered one to Safaia. "Did you see anything that stood out about them? Did they say anything?"

"Stacy was pretty pissed. I heard one of them mention Harry Barton, the fight manager."

Tabitha frowned at Ryu. "Isn't that the same Harry we were just looking at?"

Ryu nodded. "I think so."

Tabitha stood. "We should go and pay Harry a visit."

K'nthel System, Traveler's Rest, Entertainment Level

For the second time that day, the Torcellan behind the glass screen almost embarrassed himself when the doors flew open and Tabitha strode in with her coat billowing. He managed to restrain himself from slamming the partition shut but was unable to repress the small squeal that escaped at the sight of the pissed-off Ranger.

He had recovered by the time she strutted over to the desk, leaving Hirotoshi and Ryu by the door. "Oh, it's just you again, Ranger." He smoothed the side of his elaborate updo with a slightly trembling hand. "What can I do for you this time?"

Tabitha leaned on the divide and gave him a thin smile. "I want to know where I can find Harry."

"Harry?"

Tabitha banged her hand on the divide. "I haven't got time for this. How many Harrys can there be?"

The secretary gave her a look of pure disdain. "You are joking? It's one of the most popular male human names on the station census after the Big Three."

Tabitha tilted her head. "The Big Three?"

"You know." The Torcellan paused. "You don't? Michael, Stephen, and John, as well as every variation on those three names that is possible. Needless to say, on a station of this size and with so many humans aboard, it is not a small number."

Tabitha nodded. "Whatever. I'm looking for the Harry who was running the fight in the Arena…"

Barton, Ryu supplied.

"Harry Barton."

The Torcellan's nose wrinkled. "Oh, *that* Harry. He won't be in his quarters at this time. He likes to hold court in Freyja's, a bar on Level Seven."

Tabitha was already out of the door.

K'nthel System, Traveler's Rest, Level Seven, Freyja's Bar

The party was still in full swing when Tabitha and the Tontos arrived, the after-midnight crowd showing no sign of giving in to the threat of the approaching new day. The deep vibration of the music hit them the moment they entered the main room of the bar.

Tabitha pointed out the artwork on the walls of the deep galley-style room as they worked their way through the press in search of the crooked fight boss. *This décor is out of this world. The owner has put a lot of effort in,* she thought. She swerved around a human carrying a tray of drinks and moved in to take a closer look at the nearest piece. *I like the Scandinavian theme. Very...Viking-y, in a* Mad Max *kind of way.*

Hirotoshi blinked away the flashing neon that assaulted him and made a noncommittal noise. *I hesitate to visit an establishment like this.*

Ryu grinned as the bar came into sight through a gap in the crowd. *What's not to like?*

It is more how much we will have to pay for damages after we finish speaking with him. Bethany Anne was not pleased with the bill from our night out on Flex. Hirotoshi nodded past the bar to where two Shrillexians prevented entry to a roped-off VIP area. A red-faced human sat at a table behind the rope but in view of the whole bar. *That is Harry.*

I want to say "Ewww," but I can see how he manages to get all his info this way. Look who he's sitting with, and look how hard they're all pretending they're happy to be there. He's got something on every single one of them, I bet. Tabitha knew this game. Everything the man did was for show. Harry had a woman hanging off each arm and was making sure that *everyone* noticed how much he was spending. His braying laughter carried even over the loud hum of the crowd, but the laughter of the people surrounding him had an edge of brittleness to it. *Actually, no. I'm going to stick with my original assessment of ew. Shall we break this up? It's almost painful to watch all this ass-kissing. The sooner we find out what he knows, the sooner we can find Stacy.*

Hirotoshi watched the display with careful impassivity. *Nothing would make me happier, Kemosabe.*

The Shrillexian bouncers moved to block their entry into the VIP area. "Invitation only," one of them told her in that regretful way good bouncers have. Tabitha held her badge in the bouncer's face. "Ranger business."

The Shrillexian bent down to examine the decal on her badge. "*You're* Ranger Two? The scourge of the Skaines? But you're so... So..."

"What?" Tabitha demanded.

The Shrillexian held his hands up. "I don't want any trouble, Ranger."

Tabitha tucked her badge away. "If that's the case, then you're the first Shrillexians I've met who don't. What gives?"

The bouncers exchanged a look. "It's the drink, Ranger," the bouncer confided in an almost whisper. "The one from the Empress that stops us from fighting without thinking. We got hold of some, and it changed everything for us."

The other bouncer looked a little worried. "Just don't tell anyone. Please? If the others found out, we'd be ridiculed for it." He looked around to make sure no one was listening. "It's a big relief not being driven by instinct anymore. The drink gives us control over our lives, and we owe the Empress our thanks."

"You don't fight, *and* you have manners?" Tabitha turned to Hirotoshi and Ryu. "What is with this place? It's like I've fallen into some weird ass-backward reality or something. What's next, an Ixtali who likes to mind their own business?"

"How about a Skaine who is focused on helping others?" Ryu supplied.

Tabitha narrowed her eyes at him and turned back to the Shrillexians. "I won't tell a soul. And if you want something a little more exciting than this, you should head over to Yoll and see a man by the name of Nathan Lowell."

The Shrillexians nodded, and one of them lifted the rope. "Thank you, Ranger."

Tabitha sashayed past them into the VIP area. *You see that? That's what respect looks like. Now, where is Harry?*

They skirted the edge of the VIP area until they came to his table. Harry looked up to see whose shadow had just fallen across him. "Hello, beautiful. You want to join us?" He gave the woman on his right a little nudge and patted the seat beside him when the woman moved over with a spiteful glare at Tabitha.

Tabitha looked them both over and laughed. "Oh, you *wish*! We're not here on pleasure, Harry. This is strictly business."

Harry looked past her and saw Hirotoshi and Ryu. He slapped his leg in delight and waved at the table's occupants. "Heeeey, these are the guys I was telling you all about!" He scrutinized Tabitha. "What are you, their agent or something?"

Tabitha took note of the hulking guards at Harry's shoulders. *I think I'll play along for now. I really don't want to wreck this place.*

The owner of this place appreciates your discretion, Empress' Ranger.

What the... Tabitha spun around to locate the source of the intruding voice in her mind, a human woman with ice-blond hair behind the bar.

The woman smiled, her eyes twinkling in the reflected neon of the bar lights. She nodded to indicate a door at the side of the room. *You can use the back room. It's soundproof. If it does get physical, make sure you get in a few licks for me? That bastard has been running dubious shit out of my bar for too damn long, and he's too well connected for me to stop him.*

Tabitha didn't look the gift horse in the mouth. She turned back to Harry with her patent butter-wouldn't-melt smile and batted her eyelashes. "Aw, you worked me right out. There goes my element of surprise. Wanna negotiate?"

A slow, lewd grin spread over Harry's already flushed face. He stood up and waved his guards away when they moved to follow him. "Well, I don't see why we can't try. Why don't we go somewhere quieter to talk about it, darlin?'"

Tabitha indicated the door to the back room. "How about in there?"

A few minutes later, Harry was completely sober and wishing he'd listened to all the things his sainted mother had told him about not going off with strangers in bars. He struggled against the restraints holding him to the chair Tabitha had shoved him into the second the door closed behind them. His eyes darted from Tabitha to Ryu and Hirotoshi. "Please, I'll do anything...just don't steal my kidneys!"

Tabitha snorted. "You think I want your organs?"

Ryu snickered. *He wouldn't have followed you in here if he hadn't thought you wanted at least one of his organs, Kemosabe.*

Shut up, Ryu! I'm trying to be menacing here.

Just get him talking, Hirotoshi told her. *We're short on time.*

Harry looked up at them with wide, terrified eyes. "Who *are* you people? What do you want? Is it money? I have money!"

Tabitha bent at the waist to look Harry in the eye. "I want information, asshole. Drop the act. We know all about you and your little blackmail scheme. You're going to spill every dirty little secret you have."

Harry's demeanor changed in an instant. He glared at Tabitha. "I'm not telling you anything!"

Tabitha laughed. "You have two choices. You can answer my questions like a good little snitch, or I can beat your ass around this room and then throw you out the nearest airlock."

Harry sneered. "You wouldn't dare."

Tabitha frowned and looked at Ryu. "Wouldn't I?"

Ryu nodded at Harry with a sympathetic expression. "She would, and you would be glad she did by the time it happened. I would just do as she asks and hope she is feeling merciful afterward."

"Dammit." She pulled out her badge. "I should just leave it untucked, save myself from conversations with scumbags."

"Ah, but then you would have to spend that time chasing them," Ryu countered.

Tabitha shrugged. "True."

Harry looked from Tabitha's badge to Ryu and Hirotoshi with growing disbelief and panic on his face. "You... You're the Rangers? No *wonder* you two did so well in the arena today. You fucking cheated!" He began to struggle again.

Tabitha slapped him. "Stay focused, Harry. I know it's difficult to do that when you're getting a taste of what you've put others through, but today is your lucky day."

Harry spat blood on the floor. "Oh, yeah? Why's that?"

"Because I could use a dirtbag like you right now." Tabitha grinned unpleasantly. "So start talking, before I change my mind. We'll start with what you know about the disappearances. A woman has been taken, and the *only* thing I give a shit about right now is getting her back."

Harry slumped in the chair. "I had nothing to do with that."

Tabitha glanced at Hirotoshi.

He is telling the truth, but he knows something.

Tabitha turned and kicked Harry's chair so it tipped back. She caught the edge of the seat between Harry's legs with the heel of her boot to halt him mid-fall and leaned over to snarl in his face. "Never mind the crimes you've committed. You'll be facing justice for all your financial fuckery soon enough. Right now I only care about Stacy. I'll ask nicely one last time. What. Do. You. *Know*?"

Harry's reply was choked. "Stacy? Stacy's been taken? Let me up! I'll talk, I'll talk!"

"Oh. Well, I suppose I'm glad I didn't have to space you." Tabitha righted Harry's chair and folded her arms expectantly. "Go ahead, talk."

Harry's earlier bravado was gone. He sighed, and his shoulders dropped. "I don't know who took the courtesans. Honest. But I think it might have been a smokescreen."

Tabitha frowned. "A smokescreen for what?"

"It has to be all about the Loren. I found out someone had signed off on transport for it, but not who."

"'Signed off on?'" Hirotoshi echoed.

Harry nodded. "The Loren was contracted to remain aboard the station. It wouldn't have left of its own volition, but if it did, its itinerary had to be logged and it was to be given an escort."

Hirotoshi spoke up. "Why the strict protocol?"

"Those were its terms. Do you know anything about them as a species?"

Hirotoshi shook his head. "No, they are new to us."

"We've seen a photo." Tabitha repressed a shudder at the memory. "It looked like it could defend itself just fine with all those tentacles."

Hirotoshi frowned. "I am still missing the connection between this Loren's disappearance and Stacy being kidnapped."

"Stacy was the negotiator of our Loren's contract," Harry explained. "The Loren are pampered, and never expected to defend themselves. The ones who leave their world only do so if they have a favorable contract in place." Harry's face was ashen. "Whoever has the Loren now must have arranged for her to be taken. Untie me! I have to find her."

Tabitha snorted. "As if. Why would you care?"

Harry hung his head. "I *have* to find her. Stacy is my daughter."

Tabitha couldn't believe what she'd just heard. "Stacy is your *what*, now?"

Harry nodded emphatically. "Please, Ranger. I'll tell you

everything about everything. I'll go to prison. I'll stand in front of the Empress herself and admit my crimes if you'll just let me find my Stacy and make sure she's safe."

Tabitha deflated. "Well, shit. How am I supposed to hate you now?"

"Remember that he's been stealing from the Order," Hirotoshi offered.

Tabitha tilted her head. "Oh, yeah. Still, we don't have time to deal with him and save Stacy as well. Maybe letting him help isn't a terrible idea. We can just stick a tracker in him to make sure he doesn't run."

Harry was almost in tears. "I won't run, I swear. She's all I've got, I have to get her back."

Tabitha dragged another chair over and turned it around to sit with her arms resting on the back. She deliberated; was it worth the risk? She decided not. "I'm not even going to give you the opportunity. Where do we start, Harry?"

Harry furrowed his brow in thought. "I don't *know*. All I can think of is Stacy."

Tabitha sighed. "You can only help Stacy if you put that aside and concentrate. This whole thing, the missing courtesans, the Loren, Stacy—how is it all connected? Who benefits from it?"

Harry's mouth drew tight. "I really don't know. I've been digging into the Loren's disappearance, but I keep hitting a wall at every turn."

"We found your files, so we know the fights are just a cover. Why were you investigating in the first place?"

"Well, I am an information broker. It's kind of what I do. I came across the initial transaction and wondered why

I hadn't been cut in on whatever it was. Now the connection to the Loren's disappearance is clear; it all makes perfect sense." He scowled and shifted in the chair. "I was planning on having a contact of mine come out here to assist me, but we can't wait. Not while my daughter is in danger. Are you going to untie me so I can start fixing this mess?"

Tabitha shared a glance with Hirotoshi and Ryu. "You are a despicable human being, Harry. How do you sleep at night?" She begrudgingly cut him loose. "Any funny business, and you won't live to regret it. Got me?"

Harry stood and rubbed his sore wrists. "I'm a despicable human being who loves his daughter. I get by, same as everyone else." He gestured to the door. "Shall we, then? We need to get to Iona."

"'Iona?'" Tabitha repeated. "That's your contact?"

"No. It's an outpost a day or so away from here. That's where my contact is based. But he won't speak to a Ranger. Hell, you won't even be able to find Iona without me, and every minute we spend talking about it is another minute we're not tracking down whoever took my daughter."

CHAPTER 7 TABITHA

K'nthel System, Open Space, QBS _Achronyx_, Bridge

Tabitha paced the bridge impatiently. "Achronyx, are we nearly there?"

"We are approaching the coordinates, Ranger Tabitha. Putting a visual of the location on screen now."

"At last! Tell Hirotoshi and Ryu we've arrived, and get them to bring Harry up here." Tabitha flopped into her chair and turned it to face the screen.

They were a safe distance from Zaphod's anti-tech field, out in the empty reaches at the outer edge of the system, where there was nothing to be found but rocks and space-trash. Harry's directions had brought them to a massive hunk of free-floating rock amongst the detritus.

In other words, they were nowhere.

"Achronyx, there's nothing here."

"Clearly there _is_ something. If there were nothing, we would be experiencing a different dilemma entirely."

Tabitha chuckled. "I missed you."

"I have no idea what you mean," Achronyx replied.

"There is something there. I'm picking up shield signatures even though I cannot tell what is being shielded."

The barren rockscape below them didn't hold much promise at first glance. Tabitha gave Harry a pointed look as he entered the bridge between Hirotoshi and Ryu. "This is your black-market outpost? Where is the outpost?"

"It's there, you'll see. It wouldn't be much of a hidden outpost if just anyone could find it, would it?" Harry tapped the side of his nose with a finger. "It's underground. Besides, we're not quite there yet. The landing site I gave you is a little ways away from the trading post. Can't be turning up in an Empire ship. The place will empty out quicker than a Pepsi factory during a state visit."

Tabitha ignored his attempt to lighten the mood. "What's it like down there? Do we need to suit up?"

Harry shook his head. "It's inhospitable, but there's enough atmosphere to breathe if you don't mind the dust."

Tabitha nodded and turned to look at Hirotoshi. "Okay, I'm gonna go get us some protection against the dust. You two take Harry down to the med bay and get a tracker in him before we land."

Achronyx brought them down in the middle of a dust storm. Tabitha exited the ship last and paused to pull the hood of her cloak up and put her goggles on over it to hold it in place. She grimaced as she tightened her scarf around her mouth. "You weren't kidding about the dust," she bitched as she slid down the fine dust of the dune after the others.

Harry rubbed the bruise on his neck where Ryu had injected the tracker. "It's part of the charm of this place. It gets better when we get there."

Ryu pulled his hood low to protect his eyes. "Let's just get going so we can get out of this storm."

Harry led them across the low dunes toward the hulking shadow of a cliff in the near distance. Tabitha trailed at the back, keeping a close eye on the group via the infrared function in her goggles. As they got closer to the cliff, they were able to make out the outline of a rope bridge between them and the cliff through the storm.

"We're nearly there now," Harry called back.

The rest of his words were stolen by the wind. Tabitha hoped he wasn't saying anything too important. She trudged one labored footstep at a time through the deep dust, her nanocytes working to compensate for the underabundance of oxygen. She almost fell on her ass when they cleared the drift unexpectedly and the effort she had been applying to each step became suddenly unnecessary.

"Where the hell did the gravity come from?" She got to her feet and smirked when it became clear she hadn't been the only one caught out.

Hirotoshi and Ryu dusted themselves off and turned as one to hear Harry's explanation.

Harry shrugged and set off toward the bridge. "Can't say I didn't warn you. Operators of this place are watching. Come on, before they get suspicious."

Visibility remained poor. Tabitha switched her goggle overlay to show radar and scanned the area around the bridge. The radar highlighted a huge chasm between them and the cliff face, which she could now see in more detail.

They crossed the bridge one at a time, and it bucked and twisted beneath them in the scouring wind. When they reached the other side, the wind died away suddenly as they entered yet another layer of Iona's shielding.

The cliff was easily seen without the thick dust to screen it from sight. The bridge led to a path, which in turn led to a staircase carved into the cliff face. Tabitha could see signs of activity farther up, but at the foot of the cliff, it was empty.

"This place is like an onion," Tabitha quipped. "No wonder Achronyx had trouble finding out what was down here."

"Iona is a safe haven for anyone who wants to conduct business that is likely to draw the wrong kind of attention from the Empire."

Not for long. As soon as we're done with Traveler's Rest, *this place is going to get a housekeeping visit of its own.*

Ryu coughed politely to hide his snicker.

Harry became alarmed. "Please understand that there are literally thousands of dangerous people here at any one time. Even you three would struggle to win at those odds."

Tabitha laughed. "You wanna bet?"

Harry shook his head. "I most definitely do not. I want to get in there, speak with my asset, and then get my daughter back home where she belongs." He stalked off toward the cliff face.

Ryu took point, Harry went next with Hirotoshi behind him, and Tabitha brought up the rear. They ascended the staircase single file without incident until they reached the top, where they were greeted by an impressive array of gun barrels.

Tabitha brought up her Jean Dukes, which had exactly the effect it should on the guards. "I guess we aren't staying incognito, then." She picked out the guard with the biggest gun and waved the barrel of her Jean Dukes at him. "Hey, who's in charge here?"

Big Gun's eyes flicked toward a Leath who was standing off to one side with his arms folded, observing the new arrivals with an expression of barely-concealed malice.

Tabitha took another glance at the mob. No humans. "You didn't mention they don't like humans here," she whispered aside to Harry.

"I've never actually been here," he replied shakily.

Tabitha muttered a curse. "How do we get in to meet your contact if they don't allow humans?"

Hirotoshi had a suggestion. "You do love making a scene, and you've been so restrained on this mission."

Tabitha smirked. "Yes. Yes, I have. And by the way, I saw what you did in the arena. That shit was like some bad eighties movie, and I have the video. What I'm about to do goes nowhere under pain of...well, pain." She pushed through the mob and flounced toward the Leath without a care.

The Leath stared down at Tabitha with complete contempt. "What do you want, human? Your kind are not welcome here."

"Well, I was hoping to commit a crime today, and I heard Iona was the place to do that. I wasn't expecting this warm welcome, though." Tabitha put a hand on her hip and tilted her chin, returning the boss's stare with a cold-eyed appraisal of her own. "I hate—and I mean *hate*—speciesism. It's a deal breaker for me, I'm afraid. I thought it would be the war that prevented us from having a civilized discussion, but I can tell you now that we aren't going to see eye to eye on this."

Tabitha's nonchalant attitude was confusing the hell out of the guards. She smirked at the boss and waved a hand at the baffled guards. "I mean, humans commit crime too. Who are you to deny me the opportunity to get a slice of this?" She scowled at the Leath and turned to the guards. "Do you know what you're missing out on? Humans are the best."

"You *would* say that," a voice called.

Tabitha twinkled at the guards. "All I want is to hide out on Iona and do a little business where the Empress can't see what I'm doing. My credits are as good as anyone else's. Now, are you going to let me in?"

K'nthel System, Iona

Harry followed at Tabitha's heels as they crossed under the enormous carved stone pillars supporting the entrance and headed into the atrium of the trading post. Every inch of the cavern was carved with what Tabitha decided to call "space scrimshaw," including the hard to reach places between the access to the upper and lower levels.

Tabitha ran a hand down the nearest wall. "This place has a distinct Indiana Jones feel—kind of *Temple of Doom*-y. I like it."

The others looked at her blankly except Ryu, who made a face.

Tabitha shrugged. "Never mind. Where are we meeting your contact?"

Harry pulled back his sleeve to show Tabitha his wrist holo. "I gave all the info to Achronyx."

I'm sending your route map now.

The map came up in Tabitha's HUD, complete with directions to a small café on the lower level. *Thanks, Achronyx.* She twirled a finger in the air and headed for the passage that would take them there. "Let's go."

The cavern at the end of the passage opened up into a massive space filled with everything from shabby stalls and rows of roughly-constructed shacks selling contraband to shining storefronts with bright holosignage advertising their services.

Tabitha took note of the ones proclaiming violence for hire. *Achronyx, pay special attention to the flashiest businesses. Start compiling evidence to give to Bethany Anne.*

I'm already on it, Achronyx replied.

Good. They made their way through the crowded marketplace, keeping one eye on the route ahead and the other on their belongings. Strangely enough for an outpost exclusively populated by criminals, not a single person tried to pickpocket them. Sell them stuff, yes, but apparently honor among thieves was a thing here. Tabitha figured it was either that or there was somebody in charge who didn't allow crime on Iona.

They found Harry's contact, a nervous-looking Ixtali who jumped up when Harry entered the café. He spotted Tabitha and the Tontos with Harry and skittered backward, his mandibles working erratically. "I said I would speak to *you,* Harry! I cannot believe you brought them with you!"

Harry moved quickly to reassure the Ixtali, who was

glancing around for an exit. "It's okay, Hexen. They're not here to cause trouble. My daughter has been taken. I believe it has something to do with my investigation into the Loren."

Hexen looked around. "Not here." He picked up his robe and motioned for them to follow him, leading them to one of the upper rooms, an office containing a desk, a computer, and not much else. Hirotoshi stood guard outside while Hexen rushed over to close the window. He pulled down the blind and placed a couple of small devices on the windowsill. "Jammers. You can't be too careful," he told Tabitha in response to her questioning look.

Tabitha shrugged in agreement and leaned against the desk. "Harry tells us you might know something about the Loren's disappearance. It looks to be connected to the kidnapping of Harry's daughter, so let's skip all the dancing around and get to the point."

Hexen inclined his head. "As you wish." He reached into the voluminous sleeve of his robe and extracted a small crystal memory drive, which he handed to Harry. "That is all the information you requested. I'll expect payment by our usual method."

Harry accepted the drive and nodded. "You'll receive it as soon as I verify the information. Can we have some privacy, please?"

Hexen stood. "Of course. I have to be elsewhere anyway." He indicated the desk. "Feel free to use the computer to verify the information before you leave."

Harry sat at the desk after the Ixtali broker left. He inserted the drive and opened the contents. "There's not much here. No names, no locations. Where is Hexen? Has he left the building already?"

Achronyx?

Hexen left immediately and is currently in a transport which has filed a route plan ending on the top level.

What's up there?

It is the most heavily-shielded part of the outpost.

You can't scan it, can you?

No, Achronyx admitted. *But we may be able to find out by other means.*

Tabitha's gaze alighted on the computer as he spoke. *Great minds, Achronyx.*

Tabitha used a thumb and forefinger to remove Harry from the chair by his ear and sat down to work. "Information might be your thing, but computers are mine. Hexen is going to be sorry he let me within sniffing distance of his secrets." She cracked her knuckles and began to type.

Hirotoshi poked his head in through the door almost half an hour later. "How much longer, Kemosabe?"

Tabitha looked up from the screen. "Are you psychic or something?" She stretched her fingers. "You're right on time. We have a name."

Harry leaned over her shoulder to get a look. "Well, I'll be a motherfucker."

Tabitha looked up at Harry and reached back to push him away with a hand to his face when she saw how close he was. "Boundaries, Harry. Do you recognize the name?"

Harry nodded grimly. "It's not who I expected, either."

"You didn't *know* who to suspect. That is why we are here. Now, who is," she leaned in to check the name, "Brandon Tallinger?"

"My business partner, that's who. I'm going to kill the bastard! That's it, I'm outta here." Harry stalked toward the door.

"I wouldn't," Hirotoshi warned.

Harry paid him no attention and stormed out of the door. A few seconds later there was a crackle and a thud.

Tabitha raised an eyebrow at Ryu. "Did you fit him with the tracker?"

Ryu nodded solemnly. "Of course, Kemosabe. It was a given he would try to escape at some point." He turned to Hirotoshi. "We should retrieve him before he wakes up."

Tabitha checked that the copying of Hexen's files was finished, then removed the drive and headed after Hirotoshi and Ryu. They waited for her in the corridor, holding Harry up between them. He was awake, but still groggy from the zap.

She patted Harry's cheek as she walked past. "Should have just had a little patience. We were leaving anyway."

K'nthel System, Traveler's Rest, Docking Bay

They'd been cleared to dock. Hirotoshi and Ryu were remaining behind to prepare the *Achronyx* for an impromptu flight while Tabitha took Harry to confront his treacherous business partner.

Harry hesitated at the elevator door, rubbing his neck. "How far can I go before, you know, *tzzzz?*"

Tabitha winked. "Why test it? You are not going to go running off to murder your partner because we need the information he has to find your daughter. We already established on the way back here that Tallinger wouldn't hurt Stacy. Just hold tight. He'll be facing the Empress' Justice soon enough."

Harry nodded. "Thank you for letting me come with you."

She strutted past Harry and dragged him into the elevator by his sleeve before the doors closed on them. "There are reasons I'm allowing you to be present while I question him. Your relationship may come in useful."

"In what way?" Harry asked, pressing the button for their destination.

Tabitha smirked. "In that you can tell me if he's lying his ass off. Also, if he isn't a complete bastard, your being there will unsettle him and make it easier for me to get what we need."

Harry snorted. "Fuck *him*, *I'm* unsettled. He's always been an uncle to Stacy. How can he involve her in this? I'm not going to lie, it's just not something I would have believed if I hadn't seen the proof with my own eyes."

Tabitha felt for him; betrayal stung. But that was what criminals who ran with other criminals did to each other. She'd seen enough of it to know. "Harry, he's going to be dealt with according to the law, same as you when we're done. That's what I'm offering. If all you want is vengeance, I can just ship you off to trial right now. I thought you wanted to rescue your daughter?"

They rode the elevator in silence the rest of the way. The doors opened on a long corridor lined with offices. They stepped out, and Harry indicated one of the doors on the left. "That's his office."

Tabitha nodded. "Okay then, let's get some answers."

They went into the office, where an elegantly dressed

receptionist sat behind the desk talking into her headset. She held up a finger. "One moment, please."

Tabitha marched straight past through the door marked with her target's name. Harry came in after her and closed the door. "Hello, Brandon," he stated flatly.

A middle-aged human who had to be Tallinger stood up abruptly and slammed his computer closed. "Harry? What is this? How dare you come barging in here!"

Tabitha pulled her badge out as she walked over to Tallinger and brandished it in his face. "Why would you be getting a visit from a Ranger? Hmmm, let me see…"

Tallinger paled when he realized who he was dealing with. "I didn't… I wouldn't…"

Harry could contain himself no longer. He lunged at the friend who had betrayed him. He grabbed Tallinger by his shirt and shook him roughly. "Where is Stacy? I know you had something to do with her kidnapping."

Tallinger opened his mouth to speak, but Harry shut it again with a punch. "Don't you fucking *dare* lie to me!"

Tabitha caught Harry's arm on the backswing for another punch. "That's enough. Let him speak."

Harry glared at Tallinger with utter hate and shoved him away. "Speak then, before the Ranger loses her power to persuade me you're more valuable alive. *Where is my daughter?*"

Tabitha folded her arms and tapped her foot expectantly as Tallinger's eyes darted between her and Harry. He didn't know that Tabitha had no intention of letting his kidnapping ass get away with what he'd done.

Eventually, Tallinger sighed. "I haven't got her."

"Then who has?" she demanded. "And where are they keeping her and the Loren?"

Tallinger's eyes shot wide open. "How did you know about that?"

Harry got into his old friend's face. "No thanks to you. Now, *who has Stacy?*"

Tallinger shook his head. "You wouldn't believe me if I told you."

A lightbulb went off in Tabitha's brain. "It's the Skaine monk, Scroat, isn't it? I knew it!"

Tallinger frowned. "That's the part I don't know. My contact is anonymous. I arranged for the Loren to be taken down to the surface, but I hadn't accounted for it behaving like a Loren. It won't comply without Stacy to negotiate a new deal, so they had her taken, after a few mistakes."

Harry growled. "Mistakes?"

Tallinger nodded miserably. "The other missing courtesans they took when I refused to identify Stacy to them." He clutched at Harry, pleading, "Please, Harry! You have to believe that I had nothing to do with Stacy being taken. I only saw the money when they came to me with the transport job. I didn't think, Harry, okay? I'm sorry."

Tabitha deflated. "At least we know that they're on Zaphod somewhere. It's a start."

"I can narrow it down some for you," Tallinger supplied hesitantly. "I have a copy of the transport log for the journey." He held out his wrist-holo, and Harry touched his to it to transfer the data. He gave Harry a beseeching look as he turned to leave. "Harry, please…"

Harry spun back and punched Tallinger again. "Don't."

Tabitha grabbed Harry by the arm and steered him out

of the office. They strode past the speechless receptionist and back out to the elevator in the corridor.

Harry tapped his wrist-holo. "Sending the log to the *Achronyx* now."

Got it, Hirotoshi informed them a moment later. *Harry's leash has been altered to allow him freedom of the station. If he tries to leave, zap. Station security will be there to pick Tallinger up in thirty seconds.*

Tabitha turned to Harry. "You can go home."

Harry tilted his head in confusion. "But... No, I'm coming with you."

Tabitha shook her head and turned to leave. "This is Ranger business. Don't try to leave the station. You won't enjoy the result."

Harry rubbed his neck. "No, I won't. All I ask is that you bring my daughter home, Ranger."

Tabitha strode away with her cloak billowing around her. "That's my intention."

K'nthel System, Traveler's Rest, QBS *Achronyx*, Bridge

"Again?" The station traffic controller stuttered her surprise. "You Rangers don't sit still for a minute. Where are you going this time?"

"Down to the planet," Tabitha replied.

The controller sucked in a breath. "Ooh, I don't see that you have clearance to go to the surface."

Tabitha took her feet off the console and got up out of her chair to give herself the relevant permission. Her fingers flowed over the keys as she spoke. "What do you mean, we haven't got clearance? I'm a Ranger; there's nowhere in the Empire I don't have clearance to be. Check again."

The controller came back a moment later sounding a little embarrassed. "So sorry, Ranger, my mistake. I'm sending your approval now. Have a safe flight."

Tabitha cut the connection and went to find Hirotoshi while the autopilot took care of the transit. She found him in the galley preparing a meal for the three of them.

Hirotoshi inclined his head as she entered the galley. She took a stool across from him at the counter and stole a pea pod. "What are you making?"

Hirotoshi indicated the pan of vegetables on the burner. "Lunch."

Tabitha wrinkled her nose. "It smells good. Doesn't look like something humans should eat, though."

Hirotoshi raised an eyebrow. "May I remind you of our first meal aboard this station?"

Tabitha snickered. "That was Ryu's payback for ratting me out to Barnabas. Besides, it wasn't horrible."

"It was. And if it was payback for Ryu, why did I also have to eat it?"

Tabitha snagged another pea pod. "Because your face was just priceless!"

Hirotoshi nodded. "I see."

Tabitha winked. "If you could have seen it, you wouldn't look so offended right now."

Hirotoshi tossed the vegetables in the pan as he added the next lot of ingredients.

Ryu came wandering in, took a seat at the counter, and held out his hands, palms together.

Tabitha grinned. "Oh, it is *so* on."

They all chatted while Tabitha and Ryu played slaps and Hirotoshi cooked.

When the food was ready, Hirotoshi brought it over and sat at the counter.

Tabitha stuck her tongue out at Ryu and picked up her cutlery. "So, next steps. We'll be on Zaphod in little over an hour, so we need a plan."

"What about the logs Tallinger gave us. Were they helpful?"

Tabitha half-shrugged. "Kind of. We know where we're going, but not what we'll find when we get there. Well, I know what we're going to find, but neither of you wants to listen to the voice of reason."

Ryu choked on the bite he was in the middle of swallowing.

Hirotoshi leaned over and slapped Ryu's back to clear the obstruction. Once he was assured that Ryu was fine, he turned his attention to Tabitha. "Kemosabe, I must admit that it looks like the Order, or at least some of them, are involved in this."

Tabitha narrowed her eyes. "You're agreeing with me?"

Hirotoshi's mouth twitched at the corner. "No, I am simply considering every outcome, so whatever way our plan fails, I will be prepared."

Tabitha scowled. "What makes you so sure it will fail?"

It was Ryu's turn to laugh. "Because no plan survives contact with Ranger Two."

Rebus Quadrant, Themis Colony, Aboard the Penitent Granddaughter

Nickie, wake up.

Nickie.

Nickie!

Meredith probed the edge of Nickie's consciousness. She groaned and rolled over on her slab of a bed, pulling the blanket over her head as she turned. *Go away, Meredith. It's not even morning yet.*

Nickie, you have to wake up and get to the control room. The long-range sensors have detected an approaching ship. Keen is requesting your presence.

Nickie sat bolt upright and threw the blanket off. *A ship? Why the fuck didn't you start with that?*

She jumped out of bed, then sat down again quickly when the room spun around her and a thousand tiny miners got to work inside her skull with itty-bitty pick-axes. She held a hand to her head and probed for injuries that weren't there. *It's been a while since I had a night like that,*

Meredith. The people here really know how to cut loose. Did I get into any fights? Please tell me I didn't.

No, Meredith replied coolly. *You were too busy drinking the colony dry to start one. You should be more careful, Nickie. You consumed enough alcohol last night to put an unenhanced human in the hospital.*

Nickie snickered, then held her head again when the movement of her shoulders caused a fresh throb of pain. *Yeah, well that's how much it took to get around my nanocytes. It wouldn't have been much of a celebration otherwise. Besides, my nanos will take care of the hangover. It's not a big deal.*

Meredith sniffed reproachfully. *Your nanocytes can only do so much. Don't forget that you only have one energy pack left. If you get any major injuries after that, you will have to heal them at your natural rate.*

Nickie shrugged. *That's still three times faster than a regular human.* She dragged her coveralls on and hurriedly laced her boots.

It would not be enough if you were caught in a life-or-death situation.

Nickie snorted. *Well, that's not fucking likely to happen since I'm stuck here with no chance of any action whatsoever for the foreseeable future. The Skaines have gotten the message to leave this place alone for now. I'm golden, so stop nagging.* She left her quarters and headed to the control room at a half-jog.

Meredith was not done. *For some reason, I'm completely unsurprised by your attitude. Fortunately for you, I am better informed about the risks you take than you are.*

What's that supposed to mean?

Meredith brought up a stream of statistics in Nickie's

HUD. *You see? If we look at your kill-injury ratio between activating packs, you're statistically likely to have another incident shortly.*

Nickie ran her own rough calculations as the stabbing pain receded to a dull ache. *Yeah, well you should check your math. That first pack was activated to flush the drugs from my body, not because I was in any life or death situation. If we're going by this flawed scale, I still have hundreds of kills before your predicted event.*

Well, maybe you should reassess your memory of the situation because without that pack to flush your system, your reaction times would have been slow enough to get you killed in that fight.

So you say.

I am only recounting facts. Deny the truth all you like, Nickie. Just be careful.

Rebus Quadrant, Themis Colony, Control Room

Nickie pelted down the corridor and burst into the control room, almost tripping over her feet in her hurry to get in there and find out if they were about to be attacked.

Grim nodded from his place off to the side when she entered. Keen was still in the chair she and Adelaide had left him in the night before, and was still wearing the same clothes. He had been there all night, judging by the dark rings under his eyes and the stubble coating his cheeks. Nickie was glad she wasn't the only one not at her best that morning.

Adelaide leaned over Keen's shoulder to peer nervously at the monitor, and Raynard was pacing up and down the control room with a worried expression stamped across his features. All three were visibly relieved to see her.

Nickie headed straight for Grim. "What do we know?"

"Good morning to you, too. Nothing much," he admitted. "The ship showed up on the sensors right before we called for you."

She went to stand by Keen to get a better view of the screen. "Have you contacted them?"

Keen couldn't tear his eyes from the screen. "Um, not yet. We've been waiting for them to come into communications range."

Nickie shoved his chair aside with her hip and leaned on the console. "Meredith, take over in here and open a channel to the ship."

There was a pause while Meredith performed the necessary actions. "The ship is broadcasting on a Federation frequency," she informed them a moment later from the speaker.

Nickie felt the tension fall from her shoulders as the level of urgency dropped. She pulled up a chair and put her feet up on the console. "You can all relax, we're not about to be attacked. Stand down the defenses and get a video link onscreen, Meredith." The screen did not change. "What are you waiting for?"

"There's some atmospheric disturbance. I can give you an audio link."

Nickie huffed. "I suppose that will have to do."

"You are connected to the ship's bridge."

Nickie folded one arm behind her head and motioned for Keen to pass her the handset. "Unknown Federation ship, this is Themis Colony. Please identify your ship and purpose for entering the quadrant."

"Hello?" the voice was male and young-ish sounding. "This is John Deblanc of Zuifra, aboard the *Briar Rose*. I'm looking for my friend Nickie. Nickie Grimes. Have I found the right place?"

Grim's pointed stare said it all. Nickie felt her face redden as the others fixed her with similar looks of shock, but she ignored them. John was speaking again.

"Hello? Hello? Are you receiving me, Themis Colony?" There was confusion in his voice.

Nickie swung her feet down and sat up. "We hear you loud and clear," she replied. She took her finger off the button and sighed resignedly. "Yes, you have the right place. You have permission to land at the coordinates I'm going to send you in a minute."

"Great! I'll see you there."

Nickie's top lip curled at John's cheerful tone. She cut the audio link and got up to go meet the not-so-lost prince at the airfield. "Meredith, send him the coordinates." She pointed at Grim, who was doing his best to look anywhere except directly at Nickie. "Not a fucking *word*."

Grim put his hands up. "I wasn't—"

She held a finger up to cut him off. "I said not one."

She flounced out, and Grim looked at the others. "You saw that I didn't say anything, right?"

Rebus Quadrant, Themis Colony, Airfield

Nickie waited at the side of the airfield while the ship landed. She was a little unsettled by the presence of the

Briar Rose, and that was before Prince Precious even disembarked.

Mere, that ship looks a hell of a lot different from the Federation ships I remember.

Things move quickly in the Federation, Nickie. You didn't expect progress to grind to a halt in your absence, did you?

No, but look at it. She could tell just from the outside that this ship was much evolved compared to the technology that had been available to non-military persons when she'd still been a part of the Federation. She wondered for a second what else might have changed since she'd been gone, but she pushed the thought away before it could sting her too badly. *It's a good-looking ship.*

I'm talking to it. Or rather to Briar, the ship's EI, right now.

What? What do EIs talk about?

Meredith snickered. *Whatever I want it to. That baby EI is no match for me.*

The ship completed its landing, and the door opened far too slowly for Nickie's liking. A figure in a spacesuit emerged and stood silhouetted in the doorway for a moment before descending the ramp.

Nickie kept her face straight, but she was cracking up inside. *Oh, my God, Meredith, of all the things. He's wearing a cape. A fucking cape!*

Briar tells me that this is one of his tamer ensembles.

I hope you're more loyal to me than Briar Rose is to John.

Meredith feigned outrage. *I cannot believe you would even ask such a question. Of course, I'm looking out for your best interests.*

Shit, sorry. I forgot you were sense of humor-challenged. Nickie smirked as John walked toward her, holding his very shiny helmet under one arm. *It's a pity he's got such questionable fashion sense. He's actually pretty hot.*

John held out his free hand as he arrived at her position. "Nickie?"

"That's me." Nickie caught a whiff of herself as she accepted his handshake. Ugh, what a day to skip the morning shower. She retrieved her hand from John's firm grip and ran it self-consciously through her tangled hair. She caught herself and shoved the hand into her pocket.

John appeared not to notice Nickie's discomfort. He smiled disarmingly. "Good to meet you. I'm John Deblanc."

Is that a fucking dimple?

It does indeed look to be a dimple, Meredith replied.

Are you laughing? Meredith, stop laughing!

Nickie scowled. "What are you doing here? And how the fuck do you know who I am when I only heard of you yesterday?"

John's dimple deepened. "Funny you should say that. I was tracking the message my parents sent. I didn't know you existed until yesterday. I just followed the message, and here I am."

Nickie wished Grim had come out to the airfield so she could rub his face in it. She scowled at the prince. "I'd prefer you didn't know I existed at all. It's kinda the point of being so far from the Federation. You've wasted your time coming here. I don't want anything to do with Federation business. You should be on your way." She moved to leave, dismissing John with a wave.

John reached out to stop Nickie from leaving but stopped short of touching her when she glared daggers at him. "Wait a minute. It's not exactly Federation business. I need your help."

Nickie almost felt guilty about the confusion she was causing John. She didn't want him here, though. Not him, and not anyone else from the Federation, unless it was her aunt returning. "You're from the Federation, and that makes it their business. Which makes it not *my* business. Speaking of, you should call and let them know you're not dead. You know, stop them worrying and reaching out to busy people who don't want to be disturbed."

John glanced around with a slightly bemused expression. "Yeah, you look very busy doing," he looked her up and down skeptically, "what, mining?"

Nickie narrowed her eyes at him. "I'm swamped, thank you very much. Thought you needed rescuing? You don't look like you do." She turned her back on him and stalked off toward the *Penitent Granddaughter*. *Meredith, get the ship open so I can lose him already.*

John shrugged and set off to keep up with her. "Yeah, I haven't checked in recently. Nice of you to come running to save me when you thought I was in danger."

Nickie snorted in disbelief. "Why should I? I don't know you from Adam."

Or ADAM, Meredith chipped in.

Not the time, Meredith.

You complain when I joke, you complain when I don't. What do you want from me?

Silence would be nice. She tuned back in to John somewhat reluctantly.

"I need help to do this. If you're being called on to help

rescue me, I think the odds are you're up to the task I have to complete."

Nickie paused while she waited for the ramp to descend. "Look, I'm not going to help. You should save your breath. Go call your family and tell them you're not dead, then you can get back to having adventures you can post on *Rich Kids of the Federation* without any more involvement from me."

She hopped onto the ramp before it even touched the ground and stormed through the door of the ship. *Meredith, retract the damn ramp.*

John hopped on after her, wobbling to regain his balance as the ramp pulled him in.

Meredith!

I'm sorry, he was too fast. Or the ramp was too slow.

Nickie wasn't fooled for a moment by Meredith's evasion. *Whatever. I'll get rid of him myself.*

John called after Nickie as she made the turn toward her quarters. "Just hear me out, please! This isn't the trivial matter you're making it out to be."

It wouldn't hurt to listen, Nickie. He seems rather concerned.

You bitch! I knew you were slow with that ramp on purpose. She growled in frustration as she entered her quarters and headed for her wardrobe. The prince appeared in her doorway as she was taking out fresh clothing. Nickie nodded at the chair in the corner. "Well, come in then. Start talking. You have ten minutes, and then I'm kicking your ass off my ship." John hesitated for a moment. Nickie shook her head. "Your ten minutes has already started."

John sat down and sighed. "I really do need your help."

Nickie took her things into the bathroom and stood in

the doorway. "So you've said. Multiple times. What you *haven't* told me is what you need my help with."

She went back into the bathroom and dropped her coveralls. John gasped. "Don't act like you've never seen tits before," she told him as she stepped into the shower and turned the water on. "Just get on with it, I haven't got all day. Some of us have to work to live. We're not all so pampered that we can just spend the day chatting."

John shut his mouth and swallowed. "I...um. I don't know where to start now that I have someone to listen."

Nickie sighed. It sounded like he needed exactly the kind of emotional maintenance she didn't accept she too needed. She wasn't going to take it on for Prince Precious. "Start with this quest your family said you were on. What the fuck is going on with that? Quests are for stories."

"Not on my world. I have to complete these tasks, or my whole planet will be at war within the year. My father is sick, really sick, and the vultures are circling. So instead of spending what could be my father's final days with him, I've roamed the sector like a damn nomad. I've killed a mythical beast, which made me feel like shit since it was one of the last of its kind, rescued a maiden—who, it turned out, didn't want rescuing—from the Skaines."

"She didn't want rescuing?"

"No," John replied. "She was less of a damsel in distress and more like their damned harridan business manager."

"The galaxy is a freaky place."

Nickie got out of the shower with her towel wrapped around her and closed the bathroom door while she dressed. She came out a couple of minutes later, drying her hair with the towel. "Sounds like a regular Tuesday morning for me. What do you want, a medal?" She scraped her damp hair into a ponytail and pulled her boots on.

John shook his head. "That was all pretty easy to do. For my final task, I have to obtain a rare medicinal plant from the center of a volcano." He explained before Nickie could interrupt. "I need to get the plant because it will heal my father and prove my worth as a leader in the eyes of the people. Then he can take a back seat without war breaking out. I've located the planet the volcano is on, but I really don't fancy my chances alone. So here I am, asking the prickliest woman I have ever met to help."

Nickie scoffed. "Seriously? I'd kinda assumed you were dicking around on a treasure hunt or something."

"So I gathered. Nickie, I have never met anyone as abrasive as you, but I have to hope that with a name like Grimes you have the skills I need to get this done." John's tone was deadly serious. "The future of my people is at stake, and I wouldn't be here asking for your help if I could see any other way around it."

Nickie chose not to respond.

John sighed and rested his head in his hands. "I need a partner, Nickie."

Nickie balked. "Yeah, no. I don't do partnerships."

John noticed the way she tensed with her reply. He softened his voice. "You do helping, though, don't you? That's what you're doing here, isn't it?"

Nickie turned away. "What would you know? Maybe I'm just hiding. Don't assume you know me or my motivations."

John shook his head. "Hiding from yourself, maybe. You don't think you're up to the task."

Nickie sneered. "Stick your reverse psychology up your ass. I've been conditioned against that shit by smarter people than you, and I'm perfectly capable of doing whatever I need to do. I just gave up fighting other people's battles a long time ago."

John smiled. "I don't believe you."

Nickie shrugged. "I don't give a fuck if you believe me. It's the truth. It's too much effort to give a shit about anyone."

John's smile deepened, making his dimple wink. "Like these colonists? Are you really telling me you're not here to help them?"

Nickie scowled. "That's different. I owe them, and I pay my debts."

John shook his head. "I think you're lying. I think you *do* care underneath all the attitude. The snarky remarks. It's all a front." He fixed her with a searching gaze. "You have fire in your eyes. You were born to war, just like I was."

Nickie burst out laughing. "That's priceless! You were just telling me how you want to avoid war."

"I want to avoid it because that's what's best for my people. I never said I didn't feel most alive in the heat of battle."

Nickie was thrown again. What was it with this man? She wasn't sure whether she wanted to kiss him or punch him repeatedly. Mostly the second. Maybe just a little of the first. It was too bad she wasn't going to find out. She sighed and headed for the door. "Come on," she commanded.

John's face lit up. "You agree to help me?"

Nickie laughed as she strode down the corridor. "Fuck, no. Your ten minutes are up. I'm taking you to get some breakfast, then you can get your princely ass on that shiny ship of yours 'cuz I'm sending you on your way."

John hurried to catch her again before she left the ship without him. "Cool. I could definitely use a meal. Besides, that's like, what? Another thirty minutes or so to change your mind. I'll take it."

Rebus Quadrant, Themis Colony, Mess Hall

Adelaide stopped in the middle of telling Raynard her plans for the day and frowned at his distant stare. "So then Keen proposed, and I said yes, of course, as long as we can have Grim officiate."

Raynard snapped out of it. "Huh?"

"Oh, so you *were* listening."

Raynard rubbed his stubble with a hand. "I'm sorry, Addie. My mind is on the meeting this morning."

Adelaide tutted. "Your mind is always on council business these days. You take no time for yourself."

Raynard stared at her. "What do you want me to do? Abandon everyone?"

"No, just don't abandon yourself." Adelaide nodded at the lines that had appeared recently around his eyes. "You haven't slept properly in weeks, and you're barely eating. You can't keep running this hard forever."

He looked at her as though she'd lost her mind. "Addie,

there isn't room for *me* right now. I have a duty to the people of this colony. If I stop…there just isn't time."

"What about us? Is there time for that?" She tried to keep the quiver from her voice as she reached for his hand to comfort him.

Raynard pulled his hand away. "I can't, Addie. I just can't."

Adelaide's heart broke for him. "We're all hurting. That's no reason to isolate yourself. I miss you." She tried to capture his gaze, but he looked away. "Raynard. *Please.*"

"Addie… I… I have to get to work. The meeting is in half an hour, and I have things to prepare still."

Adelaide let out a small choked sob. She wiped her eye with the corner of her sleeve and stood up just as Nickie entered the mess hall with a strange man. "Then go. But don't be surprised if one of these days you come looking for me and I'm not here."

Nickie strode ahead so that John had to hurry to keep up with her. No point in letting him get comfortable since he wouldn't be around for more than a beat.

She pushed open the door of the mess hall and went inside without waiting for him.

Adelaide and Raynard were clearly in the middle of something. She looked around the mess hall for Grim and Durq and headed to the breakfast line when she spotted them sitting with Keen.

"This place is nice," John remarked as he joined her. "I'd

love to know how a Yollin and a…is that a Skaine? How the hell did a Skaine end up living with humans?"

Nickie rounded on him. "You leave my Skaine alone."

John's eyes widened. "You keep him as a slave? That's extreme. Hang on, that's not why you're out here, is it?"

"What?" Nickie scowled. "No, you dumbass, he's on my crew. And he's sensitive, so if you upset him you'll have to deal with me, okay?" She held her tray out with a little more force than necessary to receive her scoop of eggs.

John held up his hand in apology. "Sorry, I just assumed." He snickered. "How does it feel to be on the receiving end?"

She ignored him and went to sit with Grim and Durq. John followed and sat across from her at the table. "Grim, Durq, this is my new shadow Prince Pain-in-the-Ass. He's only staying for breakfast, so don't get too attached."

John grinned and leaned over to offer his hand to everyone around the table. "John Deblanc of Reinek, at your service."

Grim craned to get a better look at John's outfit as he pumped his hand. "Cool cape," he marveled.

Keen was similarly entranced. "You know, I don't know why capes ever went out of style."

John soaked up the attention. "My thoughts exactly. There's no reason a man can't go questing and look good at the same time."

Nickie laughed. "You're joking? I see the cape, and all the ways I could use it to incapacitate you."

Grim waved her off. "Ignore her, John. She's terminally grumpy. Tell us about this questing. What is it?"

Nickie ate her breakfast in silence while John launched

into an explanation. Grim, Durq, and Keen hung on his every word, but she'd heard it already. She had more important things to consider.

Like...

Shit, like what? She couldn't think of a single thing.

Nickie zoned out completely. Despite her earlier protests, what did she actually contribute here that couldn't be done by someone else? Maybe Prince Perfect was right, and she *was* hiding from herself. She'd been here a few weeks. Long enough to get involved, but she'd done what she always did—kept herself on the periphery. She'd avoided being roped into meetings, and skipped almost all of the community gatherings.

Not that she *wanted* to be involved. She wasn't cut out for management. Still, although she'd avoided all that tedium, she hadn't exactly filled her time with anything that broke the monotony of the routine she'd fallen into without even noticing.

John was drawing a crowd with the animated retelling of his quest so far. She listened along with the others and actually, this time around it didn't sound quite as ridiculous as when he'd told her in her quarters.

It could have been something to do with the energy he put into his narration. She couldn't help but smile as he reenacted his battle with the beast. He told it so well she began to wish for a good fight herself. But as she'd told Meredith, that wasn't a likely outcome as long as she was here.

John jumped up onto the bench and planted a foot on the table as he slashed the air wildly with his imaginary sword.

It *did* look like fun.

Nickie scowled as she ate her food. Maybe this John showing up could be a break from the monotony of the routine she'd found herself in. A kick in the ass to get her back in the saddle.

A pang of guilt hit her when she caught sight of a drawn-looking Raynard and Adelaide at the edge of the crowd. What if she went on John's quest and something happened to the colony while she was gone? She wasn't sure she could handle that happening a second time. She could almost admit that she liked Adelaide. The woman had hidden depths, and her perkiness wasn't *too* unbearable.

Raynard worked his way over to John and introduced himself. "I admire your dedication to your father, and to your people. What brings you all the way out to Themis?"

John explained about the plant. "I'm hoping I can convince Nickie to help me get in and out of the volcano safely."

"Volcano?" Adelaide asked. "Sounds dangerous."

John nodded. "It is. The only way to the center is through the Labyrinth of the Dead, and they don't call it that for nothing, I can tell you."

Grim leaned in. "Labyrinth of the Dead? Why the dead?"

John's shoulders dropped. "Because there's no record of anyone coming back from it."

Nickie piped up finally. "Maybe they just decide they prefer living there and never want to leave."

"More likely that they're dead," John shot back.

There was an uneasy silence around the table. Nickie

spread her hands wide. "Wouldn't you say that's a pretty good indication to stay away from there?"

John shrugged nonchalantly. "Sure, if you're a scaredy cat."

Durq whimpered. Nickie patted him awkwardly on the arm and glared at John. "What did I tell you about upsetting him?"

John held his hands up. "Sorry, didn't mean to."

Keen stepped in to save John from further rebuke. "So you get this plant and take it back for your father. Then what? What is the point of all of this?"

John sat down heavily. "So he doesn't die. And if... If he does, the succession will be smooth since any rivals to the throne will have no grounds to lodge a claim against my own. There must be no question of my fitness to lead, no room for a power vacuum to form. That is of the utmost importance. I understand that to the rest of the Federation we're eccentric..."

Nickie snorted. "You aren't even top ten of the weird shit I've seen. So what you're saying is that completing these quests is how you prove yourself."

John nodded solemnly. "Yes."

"I'll help," Keen offered. "I'm no young man, but experience plus youth can often win the day."

"It does sound interesting," Grim murmured with a pleading look at Nickie.

Nickie sighed the sigh of the put-upon and got up with her tray.

Grim looked up at her. "Where are you going?"

Nickie shrugged. "To run a systems check. We don't want to be undertaking a mission on a faulty ship."

John grinned, and Grim and Keen exchanged excited glances. Even Durq made a little fist pump when he thought no one was looking. Adelaide had a far-off look, and Raynard looked worried.

He got up from the table and touched Adelaide's arm. "Are you coming, Addie?"

She looked up at him, still half in her daydream. "Um... no. I'm going to stick around for a while."

Raynard dropped his hand. "Okay. Well, I've got to leave for the meeting."

"Uh-huh..."

Raynard sighed and left. He looked back at Adelaide when he got to the door, but she didn't notice. Keen, however, did.

He got up from the table and hurried over. "Hey, Raynard. Can I have a word with you? It'll only take a minute or two."

Raynard could see from his mentor's posture that it was going to take more than a couple of minutes. "I have to get over to the council meeting, but I can walk and talk."

Keen nodded. "It's the council I wanted to talk to you about."

Rebus Quadrant, Themis Colony, Airfield

Nickie stamped her foot impatiently while she waited for the ramp of the *Penitent Granddaughter* to inch its way down to where she stood with the large crate of kitchen supplies Grim had given her to take aboard. Keen drove up in a pallet truck, which distracted Grim. He took a break from ordering her around like a freaking house bot to direct Keen to the loading bay access on the other side of the ship.

The ramp finally touched down. She was going to have to get that looked at when they got back from the mission. That and a few other things. The ship would be fine for now, but it would be good to get the kinks ironed out.

Nickie made her way through the ship to the galley with vague thoughts of where she could start with improvements to the *Granddaughter*. She dodged around Lefty and Lucky in the narrow corridor, lifting the crate above their heads as she passed. She dumped the crate in the galley and made her way back outside to the airfield to take the next load Grim had organized. She passed Brandy on her way to the exit ramp, which was for some reason retracted.

"Why is the ramp up?" she asked Brandy for lack of anyone else around. Meredith was still sulking.

The bot swiveled to turn its screen to her. *The ramp is under repair. There is a fault in the retraction mechanism. Adelaide is fixing it as we speak.*

"Adelaide? Huh." She peered out and saw the younger woman outside the ship with a screwdriver clenched between her teeth and her hands buried in the guts of the ramp's mechanism. Lefty pootled around near her feet, zipping back and forth to Adelaide's toolbox between the discarded parts that littered the ground around her. "Hey, Adelaide, whatcha doing?"

Adelaide looked up as Nickie's shadow blocked her light. She took the screwdriver out of her mouth and used it to wave at Nickie. "Oh, hey! Meredith told me there was an issue with the ramp." She continued to work as she spoke, slotting the various parts back in with practiced movements. "I'm about done here. Give me a minute."

Nickie smiled at her and leaned against the open door. *Guess I owe you an apology.*

Are you talking to me? Meredith's tone was icy.

I suppose I deserve that. She half-shrugged. *But yeah. I should have listened to you about John. He's not so pampered. I still don't have to like him, though.*

I accept your apology. I was getting bored, anyway, just like you were. It's a good thing you decided to join Prince John's mission. I would have been forced to take drastic action if you'd kept stewing for much longer.

Are we back to the whole you 'driving me like a meat-puppet' thing again?

It's always *an option, Nickie.*

Like you ever let me forget.

"All done," Adelaide called up.

Nickie stepped onto the ramp as it began to descend smoothly, much to Adelaide's pleasure. She tucked the screwdriver away in her toolbox and grinned at Nickie. "What do you think? Much smoother, hey?"

Nickie nodded. "It is, thanks."

Adelaide shuffled nervously. "So, um...I've been thinking. Can I come with you? On the quest?"

Nickie was thrown. "Huh?"

"The quest," Adelaide repeated. "I want to help. I have all these skills I've been developing, and the ship could definitely use some love."

Nickie laid a hand on the *Granddaughter.* "What are you saying about my ship?"

Adelaide raised an eyebrow. "Want the full repair list, or just what's going to need doing soon?"

Nickie shrugged. There was no need to get defensive. She hadn't exactly had the ship overhauled when she'd liberated it. "Fair enough. You just surprised me, that's all."

Adelaide looked confused. "Why?"

Nickie frowned at Adelaide. "You have a boyfriend, I thought you two were all loved-up together."

It was Adelaide's turn to shrug. "It doesn't look that way anymore. He's been drifting away since the incident. I think we're over."

Nickie didn't know what to say. She could definitely use the help with the ship, and she didn't find Adelaide completely annoying. "I suppose it wouldn't hurt to have you along—"

Adelaide threw her arms around Nickie, cutting her off with a quick hug that Nickie was powerless to avoid. "You won't regret it!" She turned and set off running for the airfield exit. She looked back with a massive grin. "I'm going to pack. I'll be back soon. *Don't leave without me!*"

Nickie chuckled. Adelaide was enthusiastic, that was for sure.

She headed over to Grim to pick up her next load.

"Did I hear you agree to bring Adelaide along with us?" he asked.

Nickie shrugged. "She's pretty good at fixing shit around the colony. It can only be good for us to have her aboard during the mission." She kicked at a patch of loose ground.

Grim looked her up and down. "She didn't have to come with us for that. She could easily work from here. Is it something to do with the disagreement she and Raynard had at breakfast?"

"Probably? I don't really care. She wanted to come, and she's useful, so I said yes. End of it." She ignored Grim's searching look and shoved past him to grab the next crate before stalking back onto the ship without another word to him.

Give Grim a break. I think you were unsettled that you saw something of your own need for escape in Adelaide.

As if she were going to admit that. *In Adelaide? Nope. I saw a chance to get this ship running smoothly, and I took it. If Adelaide gets something else out of it, that's got nothing else to do with me.*

If you insist.

I do, now less chat. We have a mission to prepare for.

CHAPTER 10 NICKIE

Nickie diverted to the bridge to monitor the progress of the systems check. She wiped her oily hand on the leg of her coverall and grimaced at the streak it left behind. The ship was fully loaded, and Nickie had heard Adelaide mumbling about "getting better acquainted with the heart of the *Granddaughter*" as she vanished into the ship with Lefty and Lucky carting her tools behind her.

Grim, Durq, and the others had headed back to the mess hall after they'd completed the loading, taking John with them and leaving Nickie alone at last.

Peace and blessed quiet at long-fucking-last.

She flounced onto the bridge and dropped into her chair with a contented sigh. She allowed herself just one minute to enjoy it before she sat up with a slightly less contented sigh and got to work. She had barely begun the checks when there was a knock behind her.

"Permission to enter," Keen called from the open door.

Nickie spun her chair one hundred and eighty degrees and motioned him in. "Let me guess, you want to come on the quest as well." She chuckled until she saw her joke was actually spot on. "You've got to be fucking kidding me. You weren't joking in the mess?"

Keen shrugged bashfully. "I'd be lying if I said I wouldn't jump at the chance...if you'd have me." He perched on the edge of Grim's chair and leaned over his clasped hands. "I'm about done here."

Nickie gave him an incredulous look. "Aren't you supposed to be the leader? You didn't strike me as the quitting type." She hesitated a moment before asking, "What gives?"

Keen straightened up. "Who said anything about quitting? I'm just ready for something different. I've been responsible for the colony for too long. It's time to leave it to someone with the youth and drive the people here deserve and find some adventure."

Nickie snorted. "You're not *that* old."

Keen grinned. "I know, which is all the more reason to make the most of the opportunity for some action before my wrinkled ass is ready for the boneyard. I spoke to Raynard today after breakfast, and he's ready to take over. He's been picking up my slack these last few weeks anyway. He wants to do this."

Nickie turned back to the systems checks. "You're aware this quest isn't any less high-stakes than leading the colony, right?"

Keen smirked. "Sure, but what are the chances I'll get to punch anything except a clock if I don't take the risk? No way do I want to go out on that slow spiral. I'm serious about this, Nickie. I want to come with you."

Nickie wanted him to *not* want to come with her.

"Okay, and what about the colony? Are the agricultural biomes completely up and running now? No more issues with the water supply line? Do you have a replacement for your duties there, too?"

Keen was taken aback by her sudden rush of questions. "The colony is going to be just fine without me. It's not a dictatorship. The council has everything in hand."

"Thank fuck for that," Nickie mumbled. Keen frowned in puzzlement, and she waved him off. "You were saying?"

"I was saying that they don't need me here. So, what do you say?"

Nickie was torn yet again. Her first instinct was to refuse Keen's request. She wasn't so stubborn that she wouldn't take another gun hand when it presented itself. She internalized her sigh. "Whatever."

"So that's a yes?"

She nodded and waved him away. "You'd better go get your shit in order. We leave first thing tomorrow, and if you're not on the ship, we're leaving without you."

"You've got it." Keen grinned and jumped up from the chair. "I'll go and let everyone know I'm leaving."

Nickie nodded absentmindedly, already back at work. "You do that. See you bright and early."

Keen hustled off the bridge with a renewed spring in his step.

Nickie huffed and jabbed a little harder than was strictly necessary at the screen.

What's the problem?

Nickie closed her eyes and let her breath out slowly. *This is* my *ship, Meredith. My space, my sanctuary.*

Your hiding place.

That too. So what? The point is that I had just started to feel like I had somewhere that was just mine, and now I have a ship full of unwanted guests.

You could have turned Adelaide and Keen away. You didn't have to accept their help.

Didn't I? You saw them both, right? All eagerness and puppy eyes. And don't even get me started on His Highness. Ugh, even his name pisses me off! Nickie flopped back in her chair.

Again, you invited him.

Only because John doesn't want his rivals to figure out he's so close to finding the plant. Besides, you don't want to share a ship with Briar Rose, do you?

Perish the thought. That EI is the most vapid airhead I've ever met. I wish I knew who programmed her. All she talks about is... Well, never mind. The point is that you can still feel at home on the ship, even though you have people to share it with. Maybe even especially so.

How do you work that out? My space has been invaded. I was just getting everything how I like it.

By "everything," do you mean the rock-hard slab you sleep on and the two pieces of gym equipment you've installed? Let me call the media! They must know immediately about your interior design prowess.

Nickie snorted. *Hey, I was thinking about getting a mattress next!*

Careful, you don't want to push it too far. You might actually start feeling good about yourself if you keep spoiling yourself this way.

Seriously, Mere. I was starting to settle.

I know. And you will adjust again.

I don't know. I was never good at sharing, especially when it comes to my space.

Are you sure it's not just the thought of being responsible for them?

Nickie wanted to deny it. *Maybe.*

Rebus Quadrant, Themis Colony, Airfield

From the bridge of the *Penitent Granddaughter*, Nickie watched the colonists gather on the airstrip. She left the screen and walked to her captain's chair to begin the last minute pre-flight checks while she waited for the others to say their goodbyes and finish boarding.

Durq was hidden safely in his quarters, away from the fuss of the big sendoff. Nickie expected he would emerge once everyone was aboard, and no one would pay him too much attention. He was getting better at being present, but participating was still a bit much for him in these situations. Nickie kind of knew how the traumatized Skaine felt. She wanted no part of any drawn-out emotional farewells either. They would be back soon enough, anyway.

Keen detached himself from the crowd around him and tried again to make his way up the ramp. His former council colleagues had all come to see him off, all except Raynard. Come to think of it, she didn't know where Adelaide was either—which meant she didn't *want* to know where they were. She just needed them to get their asses on the *Granddaughter* before the man pacing up and down in front of the viewscreen drove her completely batshit.

John tapped his foot impatiently. "I thought we were leaving first thing?"

For once, Nickie couldn't argue. "Let's see if I can light a fire under them." She grabbed the microphone and sat back in her captain's chair with her feet up on the console. "Attention, crew of the *Penitent Granddaughter*. This is your captain speaking. We lift off in T-minus twenty minutes. Anyone still on the ground will be remaining there. I suggest you hustle."

John chuckled as the crowd finally began to disperse. "Looks like your prickly side has its plusses."

"You'll be feeling my prickly side all the way off the damn ship if you keep saying stupid things like that," Nickie deadpanned. "Why don't you go and make yourself useful somewhere?"

John shrugged. "Sure. Where do you want me to go?"

Nickie shrugged. "I dunno, just not here." She didn't feel bad for being a bitch. Not one bit.

You know I can hear you lying to yourself.

Dammit, Meredith. Stay out *of my private thoughts!*

John shook his head. "Wow. Nice, Nickie. Did your mother teach you how to be that charming?"

Nickie snickered. "My grandma, actually. My mom's pretty tame compared to Grandma Jean." She bent over the console and waved him off. "Shoo now, I'm busy."

John stared at her for a moment. "Grandma Jean? But your name is Grimes... That would make her... Who *are* you?"

"None of your damn business, that's who." She glanced up again. "You're still standing there, Prince Precious. Do you need instructions? Chop chop, fifteen minutes to liftoff."

On the airfield, the gathered colonists were startled by the sudden static burst that preceded Nickie's twenty-minute warning when it boomed from the ship's speakers. Grim caught Keen's eye and nodded toward the ship.

Keen was finding it hard to say goodbye—or rather, he was finding it difficult to say goodbye to so many people at once. He was swamped by hugs and handshakes, and his heart swelled with the warm wishes he was receiving from the friends he'd made over the years.

Grim hooked one of his arms through Keen's and extracted him from the knot of people surrounding him. "If you're coming, it's time to go. Nickie doesn't joke. If she said she'll leave without us, then she will leave without us."

Keen grinned and allowed Grim to tug him toward the ramp. "I'll be back, and I'll have a story and a half for you all." He paused at the top of the ramp to wave one last time to the colonists, who all waved and called their goodbyes once more. He scanned the faces below, regretful that Raynard hadn't been there to see them off. "Hey, Grim, did Addie come aboard yet? I can't see her or Raynard anywhere."

Grim shook his head. "I haven't seen her since she went to find Raynard, but we still have a few minutes for her to get here."

Keen hesitated and looked out over the airfield again.

"Come on. She'll be here if she's coming." Grim headed into the ship.

Keen took one last look at the colony and set off after the Yollin.

Adelaide clung tightly to Raynard in the dimly-lit room. "This is a far cry from the storage cupboard," she teased, attempting to lessen the sting of their parting.

Nickie's boarding call blared across the airfield, drowning Raynard's reply.

Adelaide disentangled herself from the sheets and slid out of the bed. "That's my final call, so I have to go." She leaned over kissed him one last time and grabbed her coverall, hopping from one foot to another as she dressed. "I'm glad we didn't leave things unresolved."

Raynard's satisfied smile melted into something altogether more pensive. "I'm going to miss you. This all came out of the blue."

Adelaide looked up from lacing her boots. "It really didn't. But I'll be back before either of us knows it, and we can talk about it then, okay?"

His forlorn expression brought a hot sting to her eyes, but she remained resolute. Raynard had made his choice, and it was the right one. She just wouldn't be a woman who sat around waiting for a man. She refused to waste her life that way. She had her own gifts to explore, and her own path to forge. She was leaving with Nickie, and no amount of sadness from Raynard could mute the quiet joy she felt at the knowledge that she was leaving the colony behind for however long the trip took.

Raynard's eyes shone as brightly as Adelaide's. "I wish you weren't going."

"And I wish you were coming with me." Adelaide released him and held him at arm's length. "You understand that this is what I have to do for myself, right?"

Raynard nodded sadly. "Of course I understand! I really do. It just hurts that our paths are taking us in different directions." He captured her hands. "You know I love you, Addie. I'm sorry I've been so cold since the attack. I'm sorry I've wasted our time together."

"It is what it is," she told him gently, then pulled her hands away, grabbed her bag, and hurried to the door before the tears overwhelmed her. "I love you too, and I'll be back. Maybe the distance will remind us to appreciate each other. It's not goodbye, just *au revoir*, sweetie." She smiled and blew Raynard a kiss from the doorway. "You make sure to look after yourself, do you hear me? Everyone needs you to stay strong and lead well."

Aboard the *Penitent Granddaughter*

Nickie was still feeling less than hospitable, but she had to admit that the pre-mission vibe was contagious. Grim and Keen were laughing and swapping stories for Durq's wide-eyed entertainment while Nickie made the final-final preparations for liftoff and John sat quietly in the chair nearest hers observing the performance.

Keen recounted an especially disgusting anecdote about an alien world he'd visited in his youth where they used psi-trickery to lure in males of all species. "My crew only just escaped with our balls intact. I was lucky enough to have been thinking a lot about a particular woman at the time, and there was no way she could have been there, so we hightailed it out of there."

John nudged her with his elbow. "Was that almost a smile?"

Nickie glowered at him. "Fuck off and smile at yourself."

John grinned. "I could...but don't you need the coordinates to our destination?"

"You can give Meredith the coordinates. What I *need* is for Adelaide to hurry her ass up so we can get going already. Time's a-wastin'. Grim, is she aboard yet?"

"Why does everyone keep asking me?"

"I can go look for her," John offered.

"Adelaide has just boarded the ship," Meredith informed them from the speaker. "The final launch sequence is complete, so we're good to go as soon as everyone is securely in their seats.

Keen cut his story short and he and Grim got to strapping themselves into their harnesses while Durq did the same.

An out-of-breath Adelaide hurtled onto the bridge a minute or two later. "I'm here, I'm here!"

Nickie raised an eyebrow. "Nice of you to join us."

"Sorry I was almost late." She dashed over to the remaining empty chair and strapped in.

Nickie took in her rumpled clothing, hastily-done hair, and the stubble rash along her jawline. "As long as it was worth it."

Grim was delighted. "You and Raynard made up?"

Adelaide blushed and looked down to adjust her restraints. "Uh-huh."

Nickie smirked. "Then it wasn't a wasted minute. Now let's go find a magical plant. Meredith, take us up."

Adelaide and Keen exchanged a glance as the *Granddaughter* lifted off. Their eyes were bright with the prospect of adventure mixed with the bittersweet sadness of leaving their home behind.

CHAPTER 11 NICKIE

Rebus Quadrant, Aboard the *Penitent Granddaughter*, Mess

Nickie grabbed the dish of mixed vegetables and passed it to Keen, who was waving at her from a few seats down to get next dibs on the veggies. She took the platter he offered in return and piled her plate with meat.

"I hope you didn't just take everything but the greens," Grim admonished. "After I put all that effort into them just so you would eat some."

Nickie smirked and cut into a chop. "Do you see any on my plate? I'm happy with what I've got here, thanks."

Grim shook his head sadly as he filled his plate from another dish. "Heathen."

Nickie waved her fork. "Food is food. As long as it's edible, it will do. I'm just not that fussy."

Grim laughed. "If you want to put it that way."

Nickie grinned. "Food's good, Grim. Thanks, you're the best."

Grim put a hand to his chest and pretended to swoon. "All the compliments—it's too much!"

Nickie leaned over and slapped his arm. "Don't be such an ass, Grim."

Adelaide's chuckle was quieter as she worked her way through her food. "It's nice to all eat together. Makes it a bit easier to be away from home."

Nickie laughed. "It's a change from sitting by myself in my chair on the bridge. I didn't even know this place existed. I thought the only mess on the ship was the one I leave in my wake."

The house bots can definitely attest to that, Meredith piped up. *Lefty says if you don't start hanging up your wet towels he's going to file a complaint.*

Grim noticed Nickie's faraway expression. "What's Meredith saying."

"Nothing," Nickie denied.

"Not true," Meredith informed them via the ship speakers. "I was merely confirming the truth of Nickie's statement about her slovenly housekeeping."

"We don't need it confirmed," Grim replied. "We live with her. We *know*."

Nickie huffed. "I'm sitting right here! I take back my compliment, Grim. You suck."

John finished loading his plate and came to sit across from her. "This is all fantastic, Grim. It's so damn good to eat something cooked with care after so long on rations."

"They're going to miss you on the colony, my friend," Keen agreed.

Grim beamed with pleasure. "I've got to say, it was nice to cook for people who understand the difference between a meal I spent the whole day preparing and a can of cold beans."

Nickie looked up from her plate and pointed her fork at him. "I never said that. I said that when you're hungry, it doesn't matter where the calories come from. You all should be grateful that we evolved beyond needing blood to survive. That shit would not be pretty at mealtimes, let me tell you."

"Who is 'we?'" Durq inquired in a trembling voice.

Grim put a hand out to comfort him. "Nickie is referring to the enhanced humans of the Federation, Durq."

Durq's fork landed on his plate, forgotten. "Like Ranger Two? When I was a Skainlet, the older Skaines told stories about the Ranger that gave me nightmares. If she came, Skaines died." He picked up his fork to resume eating. "Not that they probably didn't deserve it." He went on to tell them about a distant relative. "She must have been feeling merciful that day since she only arrested my uncle and his cohort. The few who survived her massacre, anyway."

Nickie thought the story sounded familiar, but Durq's take on it was far bloodier than the one she'd read in her aunt's diary. "You can bet they deserved whatever she gave them," she assured Durq. "My Aunt Tabitha always knew a scumbag when she saw one, and apart from you, I've never met a Skaine who wasn't a scumbag."

Durq shrugged and looked down at his food. "That's true. I've met a lot more Skaines than you, and none have ever treated me with the kindness you have."

Keen slapped the table and guffawed. "That reminds me of the time I visited this planet full of these pod-like creatures. We came across them on a jungle trek when we were lost, out of comm range, and low on supplies. When we saw them we thought they were fruit and went to cut them down, only the suckers spit nasty, foul-smelling gunk all over us. You can guess we weren't too pleased by that." He wrinkled his nose at the memory.

John clapped Keen on the back. "I feel for you. There was this delegation that visited our planet to trade with us. Beautiful, and I mean *beautiful,* women. Every one of them. I was their chaperone while their queen met with my parents. I wanted to take them to the theater, shopping—all the things women like."

"Women all like that stuff, huh?" Nickie interjected. "You *do* know that we all have distinct personalities? Makes me wonder if you'd even know what to do with a woman if one looked past your flaws."

"I have flaws? You'll have to tell me what they are so I can try to get you to look past them." John fixed her with a lopsided grin. "It's neither here nor there, but you're welcome to do so."

Nickie snorted. "In your dreams. So, what happened with the delegation?"

John waved a hand. "Oh, I took them out to the forest like they wanted and they transformed into arachnids and tried to eat me. All I had was my belt knife and my will to survive. My father wasn't very happy with me when I turned up at the palace covered in blood and spider silk. Of course, when he realized I'd uncovered an assassination plot, he calmed down some."

Nickie snickered, and Adelaide giggled a little.

John winked at them. "True story, every word."

Nickie listened to them banter back and forth for her

and Adelaide's amusement as she ate. Grim threw in a couple of anecdotes too, although his were a little drier than either Keen's or John's. She hadn't wanted any of this, so she had to wonder why she didn't completely hate the easy rhythm they were beginning to settle into with the help of Grim's good cooking.

How are you feeling about the intrusion now?

Why do you always want to know how I'm feeling? I'm fine, obviously.

The time lock on your aunt's next diary entry has expired.

Nickie considered leaving to read it immediately. She even went so far as pushing her chair back to stand, but then a fresh wave of laughter went around the group in response to whatever Keen had just said. *I think I'll wait until after dinner, Mere.*

Meredith paused a beat before replying, *That's fine, Nickie. It will be there when you're ready.*

John leaned over with a bottle in his hand. "Top up?"

Nickie held out her glass and grinned at his slightly flushed cheeks. "It was decent of you to bring this over from your ship."

Grim held up his own glass. "It was more than decent. This is damn good wine. Of course, the sugar content could be higher, but human vintners all seem to prefer these dryer varietals." He paused a moment. "Hey, I don't suppose you have anything like amaretto in your stash? Oh, the things I could do with that..." Grim was lost in fantasies of desserts.

John refilled Adelaide's glass and inclined his head. "Only the best for the two most beautiful women on the..." He looked around, his face reddening further. "Well, on the ship. Damn, that was so much smoother in my head." He sat down and shrugged. "It's the good wine, good food, and good company."

That brought amicable chuckles from them all, and the pockets of conversation resumed.

Nickie eyed him carefully as she sipped her drink. "You know that trying to be smooth rarely results in success, right?"

John raised his hands in supplication to Nickie. "A man has to try."

Nickie wagged a finger. "No, he doesn't. They should teach you that shit in prince school, or whatever. But you can bring wine whenever you like." She lifted her glass and snickered at the look of confusion he wore as he tried to work out the sting in her reply.

John started to speak a couple of times before he gave up and shook his head. "No, you've lost me. Are you saying bring wine, and don't try too hard?"

Nickie sighed. "No. I'm saying don't try at all. But yes, you should definitely bring wine while you're not trying." She stood and gathered the empty plates. "And just to prove I'm not such a terrible housekeeper, I'm going to take care of the dishes." She looked pointedly at Grim before she stalked out with them.

They heard her mutter as she left, "Can't be that difficult. It's just soap and hot water…"

Grim got up to follow her. "I'd better go help."

Durq smirked. "She doesn't know about the dishwasher, does she?"

Grim cackled as he left. "Why would she? She only comes into the galley to raid the food stores."

Adelaide smiled. "It's the thought that counts. Come on, let's all help."

An hour later Nickie dragged her tired feet into her quarters. She'd said goodnight and left everyone to finish up in the galley, unable to resist the siren call of her Aunt Tabitha's diary entry any longer.

She activated the light and took a step back. *Meredith, what the fuck?*

Her cold, hard slab of a bed had been topped with a thick mattress. She went straight to the bed and lifted the soft blanket, which was also new. *What is all this? Where did it come from?*

Ah, yes. John had it brought from the Briar Rose. *It's new and unused. I checked before I let Grim bring it in here.*

Nickie didn't know what to say. As much as she hated to admit it, John's gift was actually pretty thoughtful. She wondered why she felt the need to be such a bitch with him when he'd treated her with nothing but respect.

Are you okay? You've gone very quiet.

She heard the concern in Meredith's question. *I'm fine. Just tired, that's all.* She changed out of her coveralls and shook out the blankets before getting into her bed. *Oh, wow. That's just...*

How is it?

Nickie stretched out and snuggled into the pillows. *Can't talk right now, too comfy.* She closed her eyes for a moment and savored the luxury. *Mere?*

Yes, Nickie?

Having everyone on the ship...it's not as bad as I expected. She stared at the ceiling, unseeing. *I'm not saying it's great, but I thought I'd have spaced them all already for pissing me off, and instead, we all had an okay dinner.*

It was good to see you laughing again.

Nickie turned that over in her thoughts for a moment. *I suppose it felt good to laugh. I'm even starting to look forward to the mission a little bit. I don't know how I'm going to work with them all, but I'm going to try.*

So you're coming around to the idea that isolating yourself isn't the way to move forward?

Whoa, that got deep fast. All I'm saying is that I want to succeed in the mission. Don't have to read so much into it.

If you say so.

I do say so. I also say it's time to read my Aunt Tabitha's journal entry before I fall asleep.

K'nthel System, Zaphod, QBS *Achronyx*, Armory

The information they'd wrung from Tallinger had brought them to a spot above one of the many temples of Zaphod. Tabitha glanced at the console screen as she strapped on her weapons.

This temple below was a far cry from the lovingly-crafted monuments Tabitha had seen so far. Even with the approaching twilight to soften it the lines of the building were harsh and unforgiving. "Um, guys? It looks more like a prison compound than a place anyone gets taken care of."

Hirotoshi agreed. "I believe this temple's isolation is not accidental."

Tabitha grunted with frustration and banged her hand on the console. "I wish Achronyx wasn't in hiding. He gets so much more out of the scanners."

Ryu patted her shoulder on his way past. "I'm sure we'll find out what's in there soon enough."

Tabitha smirked and stopped typing. "You've got that

right, I just made those scanners my bitch. Here, guys. I've got what we need."

Hirotoshi came over to the console. "What did you get from the infrared?"

Tabitha expanded the scan results to show Hirotoshi and Ryu. "We have warm bodies all over the temple. There's a group on the upper level. They're pretty concentrated, but they're moving between rooms. Since they appear to have freedom of movement around the temple we can assume those are our bad guys. There are also the isolated heat signatures in constant motion around the perimeter and grounds. Those must be the guards. Then it gets weird."

"How so?" Hirotoshi asked.

"There's a basement level, which is like really deep. All I could get was a rough impression of maybe six people and this large heat source, so there's someone down there."

Ryu scrutinized the image. "It's too big to be human, so it has to be our Loren."

Tabitha nodded. "I think so. Whether the other sources are Stacy and the missing courtesans or just more guards, I can't tell without Achronyx to assist."

Hirotoshi and Ryu regarded the image onscreen for a long minute, then Hirotoshi nodded to Tabitha. "Either or both is likely."

Tabitha asked, "Want to make it interesting?"

Hirotoshi raised an eyebrow. "These things usually end up being much more interesting for you than they are for Ryu or me."

"You can't go up against all this awesome and expect to come out a winner." Tabitha laughed as she flounced out of the armory and made her way to the drop doors in the cargo bay with Ryu.

Hirotoshi tightened a final strap and sighed before heading out of the armory after them.

Tabitha leaned out of the ship to look at the temple below and whooped at the feel of the wind rushing in her face. "You guys ready?"

Hirotoshi eyed the exit warily. "I am still not certain about using the G-bars without Achronyx to operate them."

Tabitha straightened up and made a face at Hirotoshi. "Can you not be so stuffy? We need to get down there quietly and quickly, and we haven't got Achronyx to help since the Order refused Bethany Anne's request to make an exception for him."

Ryu came to stand by the drop door with his G-bar. "I find that suspicious in the extreme. Why refuse if they have nothing to hide?"

Tabitha pointed at Ryu. "Exactly. It just confirms that everything we've learned about them is true. It doesn't matter, though. We'll get to the bottom of this one way or another. Let's go." She activated her G-bar as she dropped out of the open door.

The wind wrapped around Tabitha as she fell, the G-bar slowing her descent into something manageable. Hirotoshi and Ryu were right behind her as they plummeted toward the ground, three streaks of death in the darkening night.

They landed softly on the temple roof, and Tabitha exchanged her G-bar for her drones.

Ryu eyed the marble-sized spheres skeptically. *Will they work?*

Only one way to find out. She tossed them up into the air, and they went a little way from her before dropping to the roof, inert. *Guess not.* She shrugged and picked them up again, dropping them back into their pouch before she drew her Jean Dukes and checked it. *At least I have something I can rely on.*

Hirotoshi patted the sword at his hip. *You can't get more reliable than cold steel.*

Tabitha snickered. *If you say so. I'll stick with Jean's best, thanks.* She nodded toward the temple roof access, and they padded over in silence.

Ryu broke the lock on the door with a twist and Tabitha led them into the temple with her Jean Dukes at the ready. They worked their way down into the main complex through the dark corridors, avoiding alerting any of the occupants to their presence just yet.

Tabitha turned to them when they reached the staircase that went down to the basement level. *Just like we planned. Hirotoshi, take out the guards at the top. Ryu deal with the ones on patrol. Then both of you get back here and cover me and whoever I find down there who doesn't need introducing to Saint Payback while I get them out.*

Ryu grumbled a little about his assignment as he and Hirotoshi peeled off in separate directions

Tabitha grinned and wiggled her fingers at them. *You two have fun now, okay?* She moved on silent feet down the stairs into the underground level of the temple.

She realized she'd been a little hasty in calling it a basement. Deep-rooted vines crept over every carved surface and the frescoed wall of the cavern. The roof was supported by a double row of elaborate pillars that created an imposing avenue to the other end of the vaulted space, where a green-blue pool lay in front of what looked to be an altar. *You guys should see this,* she murmured over her mental link to the Tontos. *You're going to love what they've done with the place.*

Little busy, Hirotoshi replied tersely.

Need a hand? Ryu asked. *I've got two here that are doing nothing.*

That would be good.

Are you okay? Tabitha asked. *I can come up there if you need me.*

No, Kemosabe. You have more important work. Hirotoshi grunted, Tabitha recognized the noise as his exhale on a downswing.

I'm with him now, Ryu assured her. *Go rescue Stacy and the sexy tentacle alien.*

Tabitha snickered. *You think the Loren is sexy? I'll be sure to tell her when I find her.*

Ryu spluttered. *That's not what I meant!*

I know what you meant, she teased. *Now finish up what you're doing and get your asses down here. This place is unbelievable.*

Tabitha's eye was drawn by a slight movement near the altar and she walked down the center, alert to the possibility of a surprise attack. She reached the altar, but there was no one there. The vines swung lazily behind it.

"This is creepy," Tabitha muttered. "Not as creepy as talking to myself. Damn, I miss Achronyx." She climbed up behind the altar and discovered that the apparent solidity of the back wall was nothing but an optical illusion. She peered around the façade into the dark passage beyond.

Hey, guys? I've found a secret passageway, and I'm pretty sure I saw someone go into it. I'm going to follow and see where it leads.

We are on our way, Hirotoshi responded. *We will find you.*

Tabitha pushed the vines aside and set off down the downward-sloping passage at a light jog. *Behind the altar, you'll see the fake wall.* She took note of the rapid decline as she negotiated the twists and turns of the passage and wondered how deep underground she would be at the end of the passage.

Tabitha grinned as she ran through the darkness. Her enhanced vision meant that the darkness was her ally instead of a hindrance. She was a Nacht, a badass, hot-as-hell creature of the night. Unstoppable in her bodaciousness.

Nevertheless, it made for a shock when the passage suddenly turned a corner and her night vision was destroyed by the light of a thousand candles.

She stumbled, shielding her eyes just a moment too late, and fell backward...into Hirotoshi.

She recovered and grinned at him and Ryu. "Nice of you to join me."

Ryu pointed behind her. "Um..."

Tabitha wheeled around, her Jean Dukes up and ready for— "Stacy?"

The young woman in question was pressed up against the bars of one of the cells that lined both sides of the room, staring at Tabitha and the Tontos in complete shock. "R-ranger Tabitha?"

Tabitha rushed over to free her. "The one and only. Let's get you out of here." She snapped the lock and pulled the barred door open.

Stacy tumbled out into Tabitha's arms. "I've never been so glad to see anyone in my life."

Tabitha soothed her. "It's okay, we've got you now. Are you hurt? Did they hurt you?"

Stacy shook her head. "I'm okay, just go and save the others. The monk has them, and the auction for the Loren is due to start soon. He told me my services would be required by morning."

Tabitha grinned. "The others? The courtesans—they're all here?"

Stacy nodded. "Yes. Let's go!" She pulled away from Tabitha and took a few steps before her knees buckled beneath her.

Tabitha darted forward and caught Stacy before she fell. Stacy shook like a leaf in her arms, and if the dark rings around her eyes were anything to go by she was close to complete exhaustion. Tabitha wasn't taking her anywhere just yet.

Tabitha wrapped Stacy's arm over her shoulder. "Yeah, sweetie, we're going to find you a place to hide first. Tell me what you know about this place; how many bad guys, what rooms you've seen." She guided her over to a shadowed nook off to the side, and Stacy told Tabitha what she'd seen while she helped her get comfortable.

Tabitha paused before leaving. "Just stay here until we get back." She removed one of her backup pistols from her thigh holster and handed it to Stacy. "I'm breaking every rule giving you this, so don't shoot yourself or us by accident."

"I know how to use a gun," Stacy told her.

Tabitha nodded and jogged over to where Hirotoshi and Ryu were waiting for her.

"Did Stacy know anything that could help us?" Hirotoshi asked as they set off walking.

Tabitha looked around for the passage Stacy had told her led to the monk's hideout. "She gave me some directions, but they weren't all that clear. We're looking for another secret entrance."

Hirotoshi found it a few minutes later. *Over here, and be silent. I can hear voices.*

K'nthel System, Zaphod, Hidden Temple

Tabitha crept down the passage with Hirotoshi and Ryu close behind.

The voices drifted up from below, and as they neared the bottom, they realized that all but one were coming from speakers.

They hurried to reach the end of the passage, which terminated in a long corridor containing a series of stone archways. They peered around the one they heard the voices from in the absence of drones to assist. The room beyond was filled with technology that shouldn't have been on Zaphod at all.

The hooded figure sat at the center of a wide, curved table, surrounded by monitor screens. The soft hum of computer processors was like a balm to Tabitha's soul. Tabitha scowled at the monk. *He's alone. I can handle one monk, no problem. I can't see the captives anywhere. He must have them somewhere else.*

They are most likely being held in the nearby rooms, Hirotoshi supplied.

Probably, Tabitha agreed. *How is all of this even working down here?*

The field has been disabled, Ranger Tabitha.

Tabitha clapped a hand over her mouth to restrain herself from speaking aloud. *Achronyx!*

Indeed.

Good to have you back with us, Ryu told him.

It's good to be back, however temporarily.

Tabitha eyed the hooded figure at the desk. *Shall we find out who that is and stop the auction?*

The auction has already begun, Achronyx informed her. *We are too late to stop it.*

Of course, we are. I don't know why you would expect things to go so easily. Tabitha stepped back from the archway and considered the problem for a moment. *Okay, you guys go and find the Loren. I'll stay here and make sure you're not disturbed.*

What do you have in mind? Hirotoshi asked.

Tabitha withdrew her drones from their pouch, then rolled them in her hand and grinned. *Don't sweat it. I'll think of something.*

Achronyx, you have no idea how much I missed you. I'll never complain about your reports again.

Did you have to break into some stuff yourself?

Tabitha made a small noise of indignation. *And then some. Not that I'm not the best hacker there is, but... I dunno, it's just more fun when we do these things together.*

I will admit that my enforced seclusion has been rather boring. I'm in, let's get to work.

Tabitha smirked as the monk's computer system displayed in her HUD. *Great job. Now, how can we fuck this auction up without any of them realizing we're playing with them. Ooh, I have an idea.*

Why are you joining the auction? What's the plan?

We outbid everyone and let the kidnapping son of a camel-humper think he's been successful. In the meantime, we, meaning you, backtrack the other bidders and make sizeable donations in their extremely generous names to the Empire's planetary disaster fund or whatever. That will give Hirotoshi and Ryu enough time to rescue everyone and get them back to the ship.

Sizeable donations?

Clean them out, Achronyx. They're here to buy someone's life, probably with money earned from the suffering of innocents. Screw them.

Fair enough. Then what?

Simple. Then we take whoever is sitting there back to Yoll, and they go on trial. Job done.

What, no killing spree?

Not if it's unnecessary. We're doing this by the book; no more running around half-assed. For now, let's concentrate on keeping this auction going and do some good at the same time.

Forgive me, but that almost sounds like maturity.

Coming from your snarky self, I'm going to take it as a compliment and move on. She pushed the bid up, and kept pushing it until the other bidders began to drop out. *See, my plan is working. How is your end going?*

Teamwork is rather awe-inspiring. So far I've made transfers to twenty-seven hundred charitable causes, including the EPDF and the Widows of Merrick Foundation within the Empire, and relief efforts for the poor on each bidder's home planet.

Tabitha grinned. *I'll just call you Robin Hood from now on.*

Show me the money.

Wrong reference, Achronyx.

I know.

It was down to Tabitha and one other bidder, and it had turned into a bidding war. Every time Tabitha upped the bid they countered within moments. Tabitha grew frustrated. *Why won't they just quit? It's a good thing I have no intention of paying.*

I can't imagine you would survive Bethany Anne receiving a thirty-six million credit bill.

I know, right? Ugh, another bid. Give up already!

There was a soft snicker from the monk at the desk.

Tabitha glanced at the monk. He tapped away at a device between short bursts of activity from the computers on the table. *Is he the one bidding against us?*

Hirotoshi and Ryu had searched most of the rooms along the corridor. This part of the temple was less ornate than the rest and less well-maintained. The farther they walked, the older and more dilapidated their surroundings became.

They paused at the sound of voices from one of the rooms ahead.

What do you think? Ryu pondered.

Hirotoshi's hand moved to his hip. *I think we should go and find out who they belong to.*

They glided toward the source of the voices, a group of mercenary-looking types gathered around a table. Hirotoshi took in the situation with a glance. The Loren was in a transparent tank of some sort. There was also a small group of humans and other species in one of the more traditional cells that lined the left-hand side of the room.

The eight mercenaries were playing a card game and had their backs to the door.

One of the guards threw his cards down. "I'm out. The boss will be back soon, right? I hate it when he disappears down there for days on end. He always has that weird glaze over his eyes. I tell you, it's not natural being around so much technology all the time."

Another took a card and nodded his agreement. "You got that right, Ludd."

Hirotoshi spotted the keys on Ludd's belt. He caught Ryu's eye and indicated the keyring with a tiny nod. Ryu nodded in return, and they drew their swords and advanced at vampiric speed.

It was less than a moment's work for Hirotoshi and Ryu to relieve the guards of their heads and retrieve the keys. They got to work freeing the grateful captives, being careful not to slip in the spreading puddles of blood.

Tabitha asked again, *Is he the one bidding against us?*

Achronyx was quiet for a moment. *Oh. Um, yes. No idea how I missed that.*

Tabitha shrugged as she tried to figure out what could be done with seventy million credits. *Yeah, well, now we know. Does he even have that kind of money?*

He does, Achronyx confirmed. *But not for long.*

He definitely has some making up to do. Make sure it goes to a worthy cause, Achronyx. Tabitha snickered at the deliciousness of what they'd pulled off.

Hirotoshi interrupted her moment. *Kemosabe, we have the captives, and we are almost back at the surface.*

Tabitha grinned. *That's the sweet music my ears wanted to hear. Any problems?*

None, Hirotoshi replied. *We'll see you back at the ship.*

You betcha. She cut the link to Hirotoshi and brought her attention back to her present situation. *Okay, Achronyx. What we have here is the perfect opportunity to drop out of the auction in the most painful way possible. For him.* She closed her link to the auction, effectively ending it.

The monk at the table stood and let out a moan. His hood fell back, and Tabitha couldn't contain herself. "Cuthbert?"

Cuthbert spun and shot at her with the blaster he pulled from his sleeve as he wheeled around.

Tabitha ducked the spray of rock when his shot went wide and darted forward to restrain the malfeasant monk. She was forced to dive out of the way when he shot at her again.

She rolled to her feet with her Jean Dukes in her hand, but Cuthbert was nowhere to be seen. "Dammit, where did the little weasel go? Is there another tunnel?"

He made a run for the stairs as soon as you were distracted. I will be blocked when you leave the room.

We're nearly done here. She headed for the door and ran up the stairs two at a time. There was no sign of Cuthbert until she got to the ground floor level.

She dashed outside, hearing a ship taking off. *Guys, where are you? Cuthbert is the one who's behind all of this, and he's getting away!* She breathed a massive sigh of relief when she heard Hirotoshi's voice.

Stay where you are. We're on our way to pick you up.

CHAPTER 13 TABITHA

QBS _Achronyx_, Bridge

Tabitha bounced around in her captain's chair as the adrenaline of the chase poured through her. "We nearly got him that time. Pull back."

Cuthbert's small one-person ship darted in and out of the rocks as Cuthbert tried every evasive maneuver in the book to shake the _Achronyx_. Sort of. In reality, they were herding him in the hopes of turning up his accomplices.

They'd already given him a short head start when they made the side trip to return Stacy and the others to Traveler's Rest. It was actually kind of laughable that he thought he could outrun some of the best ship tech in the Empire in his tiny junker, so Tabitha did laugh. She laughed damned hard because she was on her way to deliver Cuthbert's just desserts. Well, his and his accomplices'. "As soon as he lands and goes running to Scroat, we swoop in and take them both down."

Hirotoshi made a face.

"What?" she asked.

"Just keep in mind that there are a whole bunch of monks down there." He indicated the map with a nod. "It looks like he's going to the main temple. We suspect that he may not have been working alone, so we might have a fight on our hands. Bethany Anne was very specific about not drawing attention to ourselves."

Tabitha grinned as the mountain loomed on the screen. "Well, as long as we didn't start it, there's nothing she can say."

"There's *plenty* she can say," Ryu countered. "'You look like you need a workout,' for one."

That gave them pause since all three had been on the receiving end of Bethany Anne's "workouts" on too many occasions to count.

Tabitha shook herself as the temple came into view. "Here we go."

They landed the *Achronyx* next to Cuthbert's discarded ship and walked toward the temple building. Before they were halfway across the grounds, the monks began to file out of the side door Tabitha and the Tontos had entered by on their last visit.

Tabitha waved as they approached. "Hey, remember us? The Rangers who came to fix your problem?"

The Yollin female they'd met previously stepped forward. "Brother Cuthbert tells us he is in fear of his life."

Tabitha came to a stop in front of the assembled monks. "What Brother Cuthbert is in fear of is facing the consequences of his actions."

"I don't understand," one of the monks groaned. "*What* actions?"

Tabitha raised an eyebrow at the dramatic monk.

"Cuthbert is responsible for the missing people, the fear at Traveler's Rest, and the missing communication to the Empress. All so he could sell the Loren's contract to the highest bidder."

The difference in reactions around the monks told Tabitha everything she needed to know. "Your order is rotten at the core. I can tell that this news is a shock to some of you, and those can rest easy." She pointed at Silan and a few others. "The rest of you can kiss your asses goodbye. It's over. Things will be back to normal around here soon enough. We can make a start with you turning Cuthbert over to face Justice."

The greater portion of the Order appeared amenable to her request. A few even turned to go and get Cuthbert.

"Wait!" Silan called. "We don't have to hand him over."

Tabitha folded her arms and tapped her foot. "Yes, you do. That's how it works. Ranger sees criminal, Ranger arrests criminal. Criminal is given due process whether they believe in it or not, and the universe keeps turning on its axis, or whatever."

Silan had a desperate shrill to his voice. "You can't prove Brother Cuthbert is guilty of anything!"

Tabitha smirked. "That's where you're wrong." She pulled her drones out of their pouch. "I have all the evidence I need, and I bet once I go through all the data I copied from the computers in Cuthbert's hideout I'll find more than a little on your involvement in this."

The Yollin glared at Silan. "Brother Cuthbert has technology? After he was the strongest proponent of the tech ban, after *you*?"

All of the innocent monks began to mutter angrily and

look at each other with suspicion. The group which had been tight a moment ago fractured into two distinct sides; those who were outraged by the travesties committed under their noses, and those who had known about it all along.

Silan raised his hands and started to back away. "I…"

He was saved from further explanation when Tabitha was suddenly blown backward by a mini-missile to the chest. The commotion was enough to turn the murmurs into a full-blown brawl.

Hirotoshi and Ryu darted among the angry monks, breaking up the worst of the fights to make sure nobody died as they made their way over to get to Tabitha.

Tabitha flew a good thirty feet, then skidded another ten feet or so on her ass after she landed before coming to a stop. She flopped onto her back and stuck a thumb in the air to let Hirotoshi and Ryu know she was okay. *Just keep that mob under control.*

Hirotoshi and Ryu dived back in as Cuthbert strode out of the temple with the portable missile launcher cradled in his arms. He had a manic grin on his face as he stalked toward them. "Where's my money?"

Tabitha sat up with a hand clutched to her chest. "Why do they *always* go for the tatas? That shit hurts!" She got up and dropped the charred robe, revealing full armor underneath. "Nice try, asshole."

Cuthbert brought the missile launcher up again. "My money, where is it? I know you took it!" He swung his head from side-to-side until he located Silan. "She took *your* money too," he screamed. He lifted the missile launcher a little more to get Tabitha in his sights. "Give it back, or you die."

Tabitha rolled her shoulder and returned his threat by treating him to a view of the inside of her Jean Dukes' barrel. "Yeah, I don't think so. Your last missile didn't even scratch the paint on my armor. Drop the missile launcher. You have one chance."

Cuthbert let out a harsh laugh. "I think I'll keep it. After all, you aren't wearing a helmet." His head exploded in a fine spray of brain matter and bone fragments.

"Neither are you," Scroat deadpanned from behind Cuthbert's corpse. He looked up at Tabitha as he stuck his blaster in his waistband and nodded curtly. "Ranger."

Tabitha caught the missile launcher with her free hand before it hit the ground and went off accidentally and returned the Skaine's nod before she realized what she was doing.

While she was busy kicking herself for acknowledging him, Scroat made his way to the nearest rock. He climbed on top and stood for a moment. Tabitha could have sworn she saw sadness cross his face as he looked at the fighting going on all around them.

She was not expecting what happened next.

Scroat put his fingers in his mouth and let out a piercing whistle. The effect was instantaneous. The free-for-all ground to a halt and they all turned to face the little blue monk on the rock. He opened his arms wide and gave them a puzzled smile. "My brothers and sisters, *what the fuck is going on?*" Scroat's demeanor changed now he had their attention. "This Order is dedicated to one thing:

providing sanctuary. Why are you brawling out here like a bunch of Shrillexians on a bar crawl?"

Two of the monks dragged Silan in front of Scroat. Another three monks were brought forth similarly, and Scroat stared down at them unerringly. "Well?"

Silan looked everywhere but at Scroat.

Scroat looked around. "Does anyone want to tell me what's going on?"

An ancient, wispy white-haired Noel-ni came tottering out of the temple toward them. He called ahead in a whisper-dry voice, "Scroat, did you find out what all the racket was about?"

Scroat hopped down from the rock and rushed to aid the elder. "I was just about to, father. Why don't you come and sit by the nice Ranger while we work it out?" He tucked a hand under the Noel-ni's elbow and helped him over to Tabitha before heading back to his rock.

Tabitha smiled at the Noel-ni. "Ranger Tabitha. Pleased to meet you."

"Abbot Dremmen. Good to meet you, too, Ranger, although it could have been on a more auspicious occasion."

Tabitha nodded. "So you're the top monk around here. Is that why Scroat called you 'father?'"

Dremmen smiled. "No. He called me father because he is my son."

Tabitha almost fell off the rock she was perched on. "Your son?"

"Indeed. He was abandoned here as a Skainlet. I raised him as my own since no one else would have anything to do with a Skaine."

Tabitha tried not to let her prejudice show. She watched Scroat work with Hirotoshi and Ryu to restore some order to the chaotic tableau in front of the temple. She had never seen anything so surreal. All her experience amounted to nothing when it came to the little Skaine monk.

Dremmen was used to much worse than unasked questions. "You want to ask, go ahead. I can see you are asking in the name of knowledge."

"What was he like growing up? I mean, Skaines aren't known for their social skills at the best of times. How did you cope with raising someone from a species genetically predisposed toward violence?"

The abbot gave Tabitha a very hard look. "I do not know, dear human. Perhaps you can tell me?"

Tabitha realized she'd overstepped. "I didn't mean to offend you."

The abbot smiled. "And neither did I. It seems we both touched a nerve. Please, accept our hospitality for the night as an apology and as thanks for uncovering the corruption within the Order."

Tabitha smiled brightly. A few hours of R&R wouldn't hurt. "That would be wonderful. I'll have to go back to my ship to spend some time with Achronyx first. He's been lonely."

The abbot tilted his head in question. "Is that a member of your crew? They are welcome, too."

Tabitha shrugged. "Not unless you suddenly lift the prohibition against EIs."

The abbot waved her off. "Oh, that. That was all Cuthbert and Silan's doing. They persuaded enough of the

Order to vote for it. As soon as I find someone who can recalibrate the systems, the ban will be lifted universally."

Tabitha jumped up and gave the surprised abbot a quick hug. "Thank you! I can help with the recalibration. I'm *so* glad I don't have to come back and kick your ass about that."

The abbot looked at her doubtfully.

Tabitha nodded seriously. "Some things you just can't let slide, no matter how much trouble it causes."

That brought a chuckle from the elderly abbot that caught in his chest and became a rattling cough. "Oh, you sound so young, Ranger. Perhaps I should not have 'let it slide.' Perhaps this is the sign I've been waiting for to tell me it's time to step down and enjoy the remainder of my days in contemplation."

Tabitha noticed that the confrontation was done. The monks were heading about their business, except for Silan and the other accomplices. "What about them?"

The abbot considered them for a moment. "We only have one way of dealing with crime as severe as this. Help me up, would you? I have to go and commit murder in the name of peace." His joints creaked as Tabitha pulled him gently to his feet.

"You don't have to execute them," she told him as they walked over. "I can take them back to the Empire. They'll be sentenced to hard time on some godforsaken mining colony in the ass-end of nowhere." She snickered. "They'll get plenty of chance to contemplate where greed got them while they're building the future of the Empire to make up for the futures they took away."

The abbot looked relieved. "Such places exist?"

Tabitha nodded. "If my Empress has a place to send the abused and weary, you can bet your furry ass that she has a special hell reserved for those who made that place necessary."

K'nthel System, Zaphod, Main Temple, Great Hall

The candlelit hall was filled with music, laughter, and the smell of roasting meat. Tabitha sat with her back against the wall and her feet up on the bench. There was a plate of food on the table beside her, and a glass of the monks' home-brewed whiskey in her hand. She leaned back and sipped her drink as she sank into the peace of the moment.

Hirotoshi cleared his throat politely.

"What?" She kept watching the celebration unfolding around them.

"You did well. You were very...sensible."

Tabitha smirked at him. "I know, I was completely awesome. And I rocked that cloak. Did you see how it flowed around me? Totally badass. I'm going to try to bring cloaks back."

Hirotoshi dissolved into chuckles.

"What?"

"I'm just happy to see you haven't completely regained your sanity."

Tabitha kicked his chair. "Hey!"

Hirotoshi shrugged. "It was a compliment, Kemosabe. Take it as you will."

Tabitha decided to just let it go.

Hirotoshi scooted his chair back to its position at the table. "Did you finish the recalibration?"

Tabitha scowled. "I'm trying to relax, Hirotoshi. I don't want to talk about uncooperative defense systems that have been hacked with all the skill of a bistok on ice skates."

Hirotoshi made a sympathetic face. "That bad?"

She looked at him with horror. "Worse. But I said I'd fix it, so I will. Are you happy that Silan and the others are secure in the brig until we're ready to leave?"

"I am."

They ate in companionable silence while they waited for Ryu to return from dancing with the monks. Hirotoshi pushed his plate away when Ryu came back with a tray of fresh drinks.

"I thought you were party central tonight?" Tabitha teased as he put the tray on the table. "Your adoring fans want more. Look!"

Ryu turned his head a fraction, then looked quickly down at the table. "Those three are a little much."

Tabitha eyed the three Torcellan females and smirked at Ryu. "The Torcellans love you! Maybe they heard about you from someone on Flex, and you're secretly famous among the females?" She went in for the kill when he began to redden. "Ryu's got *fangirls!*"

Ryu muttered something into his drink.

Hirotoshi was in a more contemplative mood. "So, Kemosabe, have you spoken to Brother Scroat at any length?"

She nodded. "Yeah, he came by to thank me while I was working on getting the tech jammers turned off."

They stared at her expectantly.

Tabitha rolled her eyes. "Fine, I admit I was wrong. Scroat is actually pretty decent, and I shouldn't have judged him based on my preconceptions. Are you happy?"

They both nodded.

"And how will you approach similar situations in the future?"

"Probably with the same amount of suspicion I do now, honestly. But I will at least consider the possibility that my assumptions about people may be a little...biased." She sighed. "Okay, what's the forfeit?" She scrunched her eyes as she waited for Hirotoshi to bring down the—admittedly well-deserved—motherlode of embarrassment upon her.

Hirotoshi gave her his all-wise smile. "No forfeit this time."

Tabitha opened her eyes wide. "What? Why? Not that I'm complaining, but it just doesn't feel right."

Ryu snickered. "You can do push-ups with me standing on your back if it will make you feel better." He patted her arm. "You don't need a motivator to remember a lesson this important, Kemosabe."

K'nthel System, Traveler's Rest, Docking Bay, QBS *Achronyx*

Tabitha had felt a little awkward putting Harry in cuffs after spending the last few days getting to know him through Stacy, who adored her father despite the insalubrious nature of his business.

However, the law was the law. Harry was the last to be tried by Bethany Anne. He'd put out his hands for the cuffs without being asked after kissing Stacy goodbye and allowed Hirotoshi and Ryu to lead him to his fate.

Tabitha knew that Harry fully expected to be shipped off to a mining colony even farther out on the frontier than they were now, but he'd kept his word, and here they were.

Bethany Anne was a few minutes late. They watched the feed to the Empress' empty throne room patiently until she arrived. She came onto on the screen from the waist down. The camera wobbled and they saw Bethany Anne take the last few steps to sit on her throne and then she was there—poised, elegant, and ready to kick ass if necessary. "Hey, Tabitha. What have we got today?" She glanced down at the tablet that appeared in her hand. "Harry Barton. Let's see...embezzlement, fraud, match-fixing. Racketeering on so many levels I'm getting a headache just scrolling through the list of charges. What do you have to say in your defense?" She looked Harry in the eye.

He managed to hold her gaze for a full eighth of a second before he looked away. "Nothing, my Empress. I did what I had to do to get by when my wife died and left me with Stacy, and it just grew because that's the life I fell into. You become the hunter, or you become the prey."

Bethany Anne pursed her lips. "Hmmm. And if you could go back, would you make a different decision?"

Harry shook his head. "No. I am what I am."

Tabitha sat off to the side, only half-listening to Bethany Anne's examination of Harry's life and motivations. She wasn't uninterested, just distracted. She'd had time to think about her time here over the last couple of days while Barnabas, Stephen, and Bethany Anne had been holding court sessions in the ship's larger meeting room.

Had she been guilty of the very same thing she was so passionate about stamping out? She hated speciesism. *Hated* it.

But she had dismissed Scroat as an ally from the start simply because he was a Skaine. She hadn't been completely open with Hirotoshi and Ryu when they'd asked about her conversation with him because she'd still been dealing with the turmoil the conversation had caused her.

There was one good Skaine.

If that had been the only conclusion she'd come to, she might not have been so unsettled. But logically, Tabitha knew that if there was one good Skaine, there had to be more. *That* was what she was struggling to get her head around.

"Tabitha!"

Tabitha looked up at the screen.

Bethany Anne arched an eyebrow. "Are you ready?"

Tabitha frowned. "Ready for what?" Harry stared at her, and she realized what Bethany Anne wanted. "Oh, yeah. Um..." She got up to pace while she spoke. "Harry has committed a shit-ton of crimes. Like, *so* many crimes. You might even call him a crime boss. So he definitely needs to be punished."

Bethany Anne's mouth twitched. "I thought you were speaking in this man's defense? You're not endearing me to him, Tabitha."

Tabitha waved at the screen. "Hang on, I'm not done. This whole place is so crooked I'm surprised the hull integrity holds. On a station packed with corruption, he's not the worst. On that note, I don't think Harry would be best corrected with physical labor. I have a better idea."

Bethany Anne tilted her head. "I'm listening."

"He should be sentenced to clean this place up. Get it fit to fund the Order like it's supposed to. When you get my report, you're going to want me and the Tontos to stick around here for a while anyway."

Bethany Anne considered Tabitha's proposal for a moment. "Sounds good to me. I think we're done here?"

Tabitha nodded that they were.

"Then I will see you after I've read your report. Stick around and help Harry for now." The Empress ended the call, and the screen went blank.

Harry stared at Tabitha in shock. "I can't. Where would I even begin?"

Tabitha slapped his arm as she walked past him to leave the meeting room. "We'll figure it out, Harry. Same as we'll figure out how to best deal with Iona."

CHAPTER 14 NICKIE

Rebus Quadrant, Aboard the Penitent Granddaughter, Cargo Bay B

Nickie ignored the sweat pouring down her forehead and laid into the punching bag with renewed purpose. She'd woken up early from a dream about her aunt and headed straight to the bay to burn off the apprehensive energy it had left coursing through her.

She felt Meredith hovering around the edges of her consciousness, but she didn't give her a chance to interrupt. Nickie appreciated the space; this was something she needed to figure out for herself.

Everything was moving so fast, and she didn't know if she wanted to keep up or run. Her first instinct was to run, her next to fight her way out. The problem was that she could neither run from nor fight emotion, and since she was done with numbing hers with drugs, the only thing she could do was face up to her feelings and work through them.

Hence the punching bag.

The chain holding the bag creaked in protest at her continued assault, but the seams held this time. She pulled back to catch her breath and allowed it to swing to a stop. Why did this shit have to be so difficult? It should be simple. When she hadn't wanted to be around people it had been easy enough to cut them out. Why did it have to be so hard to let them in now that she felt ready to connect again?

She turned it over in her mind while she worked out. There was no easy fix, she concluded. She would just have to keep rolling with it as she had been doing and work out how she felt about it when they were done with the mission. With that decision, her skin ceased to itch with the intensity of her emotions.

She stood back from the bag, catching her breath for a few minutes. And then, undoing the tape from her hands, she headed back to her quarters to grab a quick shower and a change of clothing before she went to find breakfast.

The aroma of breakfast cooking drew her along the corridor. She followed the food smells to the mess, where she found everyone except John already tucking into Grim's offerings. Grim pushed a plate and a steaming mug toward her when she sat down at the table.

"Morning!" Adelaide chirped.

Nickie took a grateful sip and peered at them all over the rim of her mug incredulously. "You're all so...bright-eyed and bushy-tailed."

Keen snorted. "You make that sound like a bad thing."

Nickie let a smile slip. "No, it's just a bit more than I'm used to first thing in the morning. It's good that morale is high. Everyone will be at their sharpest for the mission."

"It's the change of scenery," Keen told her with a grin. He paused with his fork halfway to his mouth. "It's giving me a new lease on life. I feel like I could climb a mountain."

"That's great," Adelaide quipped, "because we'll be doing that soon enough if John's description of the volcano is accurate."

Grim chuckled. "It's definitely a change from construction and farming." He stood and picked his plate up. "We have equipment and supplies to pack."

Nickie went to push her breakfast away. "There's no time like the present. We'll be at John's coordinates in a couple of hours, and I still need to go over the plan with the prince himself... if he ever drags his ass out of bed."

"No, you finish," Grim told her. "We've got this." He didn't give her a chance to argue. He swept from the mess, herding Durq, Adelaide, and Keen with him.

Nickie kept eating, turning when she heard footsteps approaching from the other side of the mess.

John walked in a moment later and made a beeline for the remaining breakfast items. He selected a piece of fruit and poured himself a mug of coffee before taking the chair across from Nickie. He peeled his fruit without taking his eyes off her.

She got annoyed with that before even ten seconds had passed. "What?" she snapped.

John grinned. "How did you sleep?"

Nickie scowled. "Fucking terribly." She saw the crestfallen look on his face and held up a hand while she clarified. "Not because of the bed, which I was going to thank you for, by the way."

"You're welcome," he supplied. "But you still didn't

sleep? You don't *look* like you didn't sleep." He paused. "I have to ask. You're enhanced, aren't you?"

She nodded and poked at her food. "Yup."

John was suitably impressed. "Are you really a *Grimes*, Grimes?"

Nickie nodded. "It's not a big deal." She prepared herself for the inevitable fanboy questions about her grandfather. It was why she kept her name to herself if she could. That shit was tedious in the extreme to deal with.

John's eyes widened. "That's... That's just..."

"Still not a big deal," Nickie reiterated firmly. "I'm estranged from my family."

John looked at her with something approaching pity. "It must be pretty lonely out here by yourself."

What the fuck? She scowled at him. "What makes you think you know how I feel?"

John shrugged. "I dunno, maybe because in history class it always looked so tight at the top of the Empire. I thought you might miss them."

Nickie snickered, diverting him from his questions. "They made you learn about my family in school?"

John nodded. "Uh-huh. So why are you all the way out here instead of living it up back in the Federation?"

Nickie sighed. "*That* is a long and complicated story."

John sat back with his coffee and regarded her interestedly. "I'm listening."

Nickie wasn't sure she wanted to tell him a single thing about herself. Then again, part of her longed to talk about the road that had led her here. She put it down to the effects of her broken sleep and decided this was a good time to just go with it. "The short version is that the Empire broke up, then my Aunt Tabitha was sent away, and I couldn't handle it. I went on a bender to end all benders, and my Aunt Bethany Anne told me to shape up or ship out, so I shipped out and lived the party life until I got a rude awakening."

John shook his head. "Your 'Aunt Bethany Anne?' The Empress is your aunt? So many things make sense now. So what's the long version? Space is a big place, and people move around all the time without their relatives going off the rails."

Nickie shrugged. "I love my aunt, okay? She was the only one who didn't treat me like something to be fixed. Everyone else, especially my grandfather—they wanted me to change and be more like them."

John grimaced. "I get that pressure. Everyone wants me to prove I'm as capable as my father. Did you ever feel like just—"

"Running away?" she finished. She made a flourish with her hands. "Welcome to my hideaway."

John chuckled. "You know, we're not that different."

Nickie raised an eyebrow. "Really? I wouldn't agree, Prince Preppy."

"Really," he insisted. "Your assessment of me would have been pretty close to the mark a couple of years ago."

"So it's not Prince Preppy, it's Prince Playboy?"

John groaned. "How many of those names have you got for me?"

Nickie smirked. "An endless supply. You were telling me about your dubious past."

He shook his head with a grin. "Actually, you were

telling me about yours. You were all set on painting the galaxy red. What made you change track?"

Nickie shrugged. "I got in a hell of a bar fight. I was injured pretty badly, and my abilities were activated. It left me with a choice, and I chose to get my shit together and help people. When I came across the colony and found out they were about to be sold as slaves by the Skaines, I helped. And I've more or less been there until now when you showed up."

"Hey, at least you're not bored."

That cracked Nickie up. "You got *that* right. This kind of action is more satisfying than anything I started in the whole five years before. Sure as hell beats starting brawls in bars just to break up the day. It has purpose or something."

John frowned in amusement. "You went around starting fights in bars?"

Nickie smirked. "Well, yeah. What else do you do for a good time and an easy fight?" She collected her breakfast things and got up to clear them away. "Are you done? We've got a mission to plan."

John drained the last of his coffee. "Yeah, sure. So, um... Does this mean we're going to stop sniping at each other? And by 'we,' I mean you sniping at me."

Nickie laughed. "I dunno, maybe? I can't promise anything if you're going to annoy me all the time."

John put his hand over his heart and made a half-bow. "Then I shall endeavor not to annoy you too much."

Nickie shook her head and walked off. "Well endeavor harder. You're not quite hitting it yet."

John threw up his hands and hurried to catch up with

her. "I can't win with you." They walked along in silence for a few minutes. "Joking aside, thank you for agreeing to help."

Nickie grew uncomfortable. "Don't mention it." John opened his mouth to protest, but she held up a hand and picked up her pace. "Seriously, *don't*."

John scrutinized her for a long moment. "Okay, I won't. Hey, do you want to train together? I saw you had a setup in the cargo bay."

Nickie narrowed her eyes. "Don't push it. It's not too late to space your ass."

Rebus Quadrant, Planet Zuifra, Aboard the *Penitent Granddaughter*, Bridge

Meredith had concealed the *Granddaughter* in a close orbit on the dark side of one of the system's larger moons. They had waited for the necessary alignment between the moon and the planet for Meredith to locate the area around the volcano and scan it, and she had rendered the data into a workable model of the area.

Nickie and John pored over the resulting imagery while he talked her through what to expect once they got there.

He pointed out a break in the jungle canopy. "We should leave the ship by the edge of the jungle and hike in from here."

Nickie assessed the topography and shook her head. "That's like forty-five klicks away, and over rough terrain. I can handle that, no worries, but I'm not sure anyone else can, apart from Grim." She indicated a place near a wide river that was half the distance and on a more forgiving plane. "What about here, and then we can travel the river instead of feeding the mosquitos while we trek through the jungle?"

"There are no mosquitos here," John told her. "What we face are bigger and angrier."

Nickie smirked. "Of course we do. So, we go in here and up the river, and if that doesn't work out, we can just hike the twenty klicks to the volcano. Then we get through your labyrinth and get the plant. No sweat." She saw a slight shimmer in the air above the volcano. "Is it active?"

John zoomed in on the caldera. "Yes. That's why we should leave the ship out of harm's way—so Meredith can fly in if it erupts."

Nickie looked at the sleeping death trap. "Meredith, how often does the volcano erupt?"

"One moment," Meredith replied. "Around once every decade, according to local records. There was an instance of two eruptions within a couple of years of each other around eighty years ago."

Nickie didn't like the look of the volcano at all. She glanced at the rising heat above the ragged basin and turned back to John. "How long since the last eruption?"

John shrugged. "Ten years ago, give or take."

"Why am I not surprised? Just our luck. Meredith, can we get imaging of the inside the volcano?"

"Unfortunately not," Meredith replied. "With Federation technology, yes. This ship is rather lacking in that department, however."

John headed for the door. "I need a few things from my quarters." He returned a few minutes later with a small crate, which he set down by Nickie's chair. "This should help," he told her as he retrieved a handheld device from his pocket and plugged it into the console.

"What is it?" Nickie asked.

"My treasure map. Meredith, would you open the file X Marks the Spot, please?"

"Certainly, Your Highness," Meredith replied.

Nickie blew a mental raspberry at Meredith. *Suck-up.*

The previous image was replaced with a heavily annotated three-dimensional representation of the interior of the volcano.

"Thank you, Meredith." John swiped the image to hide his notes and zoomed in on a craggy opening in the base of the rock. "This is the main entrance."

"The main entrance? That makes it sound like a place people visit."

John nodded. "It's a spiritual site for some. It's where our warriors are forged; they go there to be tested and prove their worth. Just the outer chambers of the labyrinth, of course. Any deeper and they tend not to come back...as we've said."

Nickie raised an eyebrow. "That sounds... Um, how exactly do they do that?"

"I'm not exactly sure about that part," he admitted. "I do know there are a series of tests, like I said, and they're specific to the warrior. All my research indicated that I'd find out when I got there."

She flopped into her chair and put one boot on the console. "That's not much to go on. What *do* you know?"

He swiped at the map again and the view of the outside blurred and refocused into what looked a lot like the inside of an ant nest to Nickie.

"Shit, when you said it was a labyrinth, I expected a labyrinth, but that's a fucking *labyrinth*." The tunnels began to branch almost as soon as the entrance opened up into the cave beyond, and pretty soon after that, the layout lost any semblance of logic. The tunnels twisted and turned, converged, and looped around and inexorably down until they all ended abruptly in a cavern deep underground. "Where's our objective? And how the shiny fuck are we supposed to find our way through that?"

John grinned. "That's where my research comes in." He tapped his device, and a layer of scribbles was superimposed over the maze. "This is just the first section. It's all the recorded routes taken by scholars and failed questers. I spent some time talking with a professor who claimed to have made it this far." He pointed at the cutoff point. "I have no idea what comes after this, but the inner chambers lie somewhere beyond here."

"There's no information?"

John shook his head. "No. No one who made it past this point has ever returned to tell the tale. I can only assume that they didn't survive the tests."

Nickie frowned in thought. "Who set these tests up in the first place?"

John held up his hands and shrugged. "It's all lost to legend. Nobody knows for sure since no one has ever come back, remember?"

Nickie couldn't believe what she was hearing. "So we have no idea what we're actually walking into?"

"Nope. All on faith." John left his handheld on the console and went over to kneel by the crate he'd brought. "Well, faith, and some pretty cool tech."

Nickie snorted. "I sure hope your tech's awesome. Faith isn't going to get us very far in that heat."

John opened the crate. "I've got that covered. Actually, it was while I was on the trading outpost picking these up that the *Briar Rose* intercepted the message to you." He pulled out a shiny hooded coverall and held it up to show her.

Nickie's voice held faint alarm. "Were you planning on going disco-dancing afterward or something?"

John frowned, then chuckled when he saw the sideways look she was giving the silvered fabric. "Oh, no. They're cutting-edge heat-resistant suits. I had extra made anyway since I was already looking for help, so everyone may as well use them. This one can be made to fit a Yollin, maybe."

Nickie nodded. "Good idea. Is there anything else you think I should know before we get going?"

John thought for a moment, then shook his head. "I don't think so."

Nickie got up from her chair. "Then we're good to get started. Meredith, call the others to the bridge. We should get the briefing underway."

CHAPTER 15 NICKIE

Rebus Quadrant, Planet Zuifra, Reinek

Durq, glad to be remaining on board, waved to the group from the top of the ramp. "Be careful!" he called in a trembling voice. "We'll be here if you need us."

Nickie adjusted the considerable weight of her pack and then set off toward the tree line with Grim by her side. John followed, with Adelaide and Keen taking the rear to keep their eyes on the group.

They watched as the *Granddaughter* took off to wait in the lower atmosphere in case the group needed a rapid pickup and then marched into the jungle single-file.

Nickie spat the sand out of her mouth. "What's with the climate here? That's a jungle, I'm breathing sand, and it's hot as all fuck."

Adelaide looked around with wide eyes. "The wind, it's so hot! It feels almost alive."

Keen offered an explanation. "It must be the volcanic system here. Most of the planet looked sandy from those schematics, but the volcanoes enrich the soil and make the abundance of life here possible. Of course, whatever lives or grows here has to be tough. When the volcano erupts, it wipes out everything in its blast radius."

"Speaking of things that live here, keep your eyes peeled," Nickie quipped as she and Grim broke a path through the thick foliage with the machetes they'd brought for the purpose. "John tells me there are giant mosquitos here."

"I wasn't joking about those," John called from behind her.

Nickie laughed. "How far are we from the river?"

"About three klicks," John replied. "We keep on in this direction, and then we have easy sailing all the way to the volcano."

"As long as we don't fall victim to the mosquitos," Grim chipped in.

John chuckled. "Yeah, that."

They made good time through the jungle and heard the water a good twenty minutes before they came to the source. They stopped for a brief rest and a quick drink before continuing on to the looming volcano in the near distance.

Nickie's enhanced eyesight gave her a clearer view of what awaited them. The peak was obscured by a low-hanging cloudbank that descended to meet the spray that rose from a drop in the river as it coursed around the base of the volcano.

Nickie looked down the steep incline to the rushing waters below. "I'd love to know your idea of choppy waters if this is your 'easy sailing.'"

John sucked in a breath. "I've never actually been here.

All I had was second-hand stories to go on. This isn't what *I* was expecting, either."

Nickie shrugged unconcernedly. "At least there's something like a drop pool at the bottom of the volcano. We should be okay."

The others came to stand beside her.

Adelaide's face drained of color as she contemplated the river. "I don't know if this is such a good idea. It didn't look this fast on the map." She looked at the inflatable raft they'd brought along for the journey. "Is the raft even going to be able to handle that?"

Keen patted her on the shoulder and grabbed the rope to pull the raft toward the water's edge. "There's only one way to find out."

"I don't know," she replied. "Maybe I should have stayed on the ship with Durq. This is a lot more dangerous than I thought it was going to be."

Grim came to stand beside her. "Can I tell you a secret?"

Adelaide nodded distractedly. "Of course."

Grim dropped his voice. "I'm afraid of heights. Terrified, in fact."

Adelaide frowned. "But there are definitely going to be heights involved here. Why did you come then?"

Grim gazed at the volcano with a far-off expression. "Because it's a challenge. Because it's there, and a man's life will be saved if this mission is successful."

"Not to mention the war that won't happen," John added.

Nickie noticed that Keen was having trouble, so she took the rope from him and dragged the raft to the water. "If we could all get our asses into the raft before the volcano erupts and burns us all to cinders, that would be fantastic."

They all piled in and pushed off with their oars. The current took the raft immediately. They were propelled along at high speed, only just able to keep the raft upright in the churning rapids.

Nickie whooped as she pushed her oar against a rock to avoid the raft hitting it. "This is a hell of a lot faster than walking!"

Grim leaned out a little to steer them around a cluster of floating logs. "How long until we hit the pool?"

How long, Meredith?

Approximately six minutes. But Nickie—

Hang on, Meredith, there's something ahead.

That's what I was about to tell you. The pool is at the bottom of a thirty-foot waterfall.

"Tie yourselves off!" she yelled. "Quickly. There's a drop coming."

They all hustled to secure themselves to the raft. The spray from the river got thicker the closer they got to the edge of the waterfall, obscuring their view. It was a tense minute or two as the questers waited for the fall.

They hit a log, or a log hit them, and the raft was suddenly unsupported in the air. Adrenaline stretched the second before it plummeted into an eternity for Nickie. She saw the individual reactions of everyone on the raft. Grim's face was set in resigned determination, John's and Keen's held an equal amount of joy, which she suspected was mirrored on her own, Adelaide's eyes were screwed shut as she clung to the side of the raft with everything she had.

The impact with the water threw them all to the ends of their tethers. Grim's snapped, but he was an adept swimmer and trod water while he checked to see if any of the others needed help.

Only Adelaide remained on the raft. Nickie checked on her first, then swam back and hauled herself in. The others climbed back in, and they paddled to the edge of the pool.

They clambered onto the sandy shore and shook off what water they could before heading in single file once more toward the base of the volcano.

Rebus Quadrant, Planet Zuifra, Reinek, Base of Volcano

Keen fell toward the back of the group as the air became thinner. They'd climbed the lower slopes of the volcano with ease, and the ledge halfway up that John had insisted they aim for was within sight.

As they neared the end of their climb, John strode ahead. "We'll find the plant growing somewhere in the center chambers, where the soil is rich enough in sulfur for it to grow. All we have to do is get there in one piece."

Nickie hauled herself over the ledge and turned to help Adelaide scramble over. "We made it to the tunnel entrance," she called over the edge.

Adelaide unhooked the rope that attached her to Nickie and went to peer nervously into the dark entrance. "This isn't the entrance we looked at on the map."

John made it to the ledge and knelt to help Grim. "There's a verified route from this entrance. It's the safer choice."

Keen puffed as he reached the edge and accepted

Grim's and John's help to gain the ledge. "Is it supposed to be this hot?" He checked his suit readout and gasped. "That's pretty damn high!" There was a low, deep rumble beneath their feet, and an explosion of beating wings came from the trees below as the birds took flight in fear. "Is it safe? I can't see these suits protecting us from much more than the temperature."

John pulled the hood of his suit up and locked the flexible faceplate in place. "It's a volcano, Keen. What do you think?" He strode into the tunnel entrance with more than a little swagger in his step.

Nickie wrinkled her nose at the smell of sulfur that hung in the air. "It's definitely not going to be safe if we waste time talking," she remarked, pulling her own hood up. She switched on her flashlight and headed into the tunnel after John. "Just be careful, and you won't get hurt."

The dank tunnel ahead was lit only by John's handheld device. Nickie hurried to catch up with him as the others followed with varying amounts of reluctance.

John led them through the labyrinth, ever down toward the center of the volcano. The tunnels were rough and almost impassable in some places. They picked their way through, carefully navigating the frequent rockfalls they came across while they followed the uncertain directions John had compiled.

The temperature rose steadily the deeper they ventured into the tunnels until even Nickie was glad of her suit's protection despite the nanocytes that regulated her body temperature. She glanced at Keen, whose faceplate was now foggy from the sheer amount of sweat pouring off him.

"You okay?" she asked.

Keen nodded and pressed on.

They came to a larger rockfall, and this one blocked the tunnel. They began to look around for a way through. John opened his handheld and tried to find an alternative route. He swiped and tapped at it a couple of times, and frowned when it didn't respond. He banged it against his hand in frustration.

Nickie shone her flashlight over the cave-in. "Is there another way around?"

John held up the device to show her. "Not one that I know for certain we can trust, especially now this thing isn't working properly. We'll have to dig through."

Nickie shrugged. "Then let's get to digging. Just wait while Meredith tells me where the best place to break through is. We don't want to get killed because we took the wrong boulder out and collapsed the whole thing."

"Good thinking."

Meredith directed Nickie to a relatively safe place, and they got to work clearing a path. They were almost through when another rumble froze them in their tracks.

Nickie paused in the act of passing back the chunk of rock she'd just pried loose. "That tremor was stronger than the last one."

"We're a lot closer to the center," John informed them. He held up his map device. "I got it working again. We're almost at the end of this section of the labyrinth."

"Oh, thank fuck for that," Nickie exclaimed. She almost lost her footing on the loose scree but caught herself using the rock in her hands as a counterweight to regain her balance.

John scrambled up. "Here, let me help with that."

Nickie handed him the rock without a word. The corner of her mouth lifted when John tried to hide his surprise at the weight. "What, no argument?"

Nickie smirked and tore a boulder twice as large from the rockfall with ease. There was the hint of a dull red glow in the space vacated by the rock. "Hey, I see the other side!" She skipped down the side of the rockfall to dump the boulder safely at the bottom and turned to climb up again.

John was still standing there with the rock in his hands and a look of shock on his face.

"What?" Nickie demanded. "Do I look like a fucking damsel?"

"At no point did I say you did," John countered. He gave her his usual easy grin and ducked through the hole. "Damsels are rarer than dragon's teeth these days."

Grim watched the exchange with more than a little confusion. "Are you two flirting or arguing?" he asked.

"Yes," came John's reply.

Reinek, Labyrinth of the Dead

The temperature rose to even more uncomfortable levels on the other side of the rockfall.

Nickie ducked through, followed by Adelaide. Then the two women helped Grim and John through the hole, and finally Keen. They climbed down the loose slope and paused to take stock of their surroundings.

They were in a larger tunnel which led off toward the source of the faint red glow. *That's not fucking sinister or anything.*

We are approaching an aperture, I suspect.

Adelaide and Keen began to cough as the group deliberated on which way to go next.

Nickie felt a little lightheaded for a moment until her nanocytes got to work to filter the impurities out of the air. "Everyone, get your respirators in. There's something funky in the air."

Adelaide coughed again, harder this time. "Mine isn't working." She swayed a little as the bad air began to affect her, and Keen rushed to steady her before she stumbled and fell. He lowered her gently to the floor. Nickie undid her faceplate, removed her respirator from where it hung around her neck, and quickly sealed it shut again.

"You need that," Adelaide protested between hitched breaths.

Nickie took a deep breath to show Adelaide that she wasn't affected by the toxicity. "Nope, see? I'm okay without it." She handed the respirator to Adelaide and waited impatiently for her to switch them out.

Adelaide gave them a thumbs-up a minute later as the respirator cleared her lungs. She got to her feet as the color returned to her face.

Nickie stalked off as soon as Adelaide was functional again, determined not to waste another minute. She gave John a little shove as she passed him. "You can quit thinking we're flirting. Unless you get off on disappointment; then you're golden. Just leave me out of it."

She didn't wait for him to reply. She moved onwards to scout ahead and make sure their route was clear, using the copy of John's map she'd had Meredith upload to her HUD. They were getting close to the end of the mapped area now, and she wanted to see what they were facing next without anyone seeing her reaction. It would also give her time to think of how to tackle it while the others caught up.

Is it getting hotter?

It is. Your suit is operating at optimum levels. I can divert a little more energy to your nanocytes to compensate if you need me to, but it should be a last resort.

She dialed up her suit's temperature control. *The suit is fine. I'll save my energy since we don't know what's ahead.*

The tunnel widened as she walked, opening up until Nickie found herself in an enormous cavern. The expansive walls were lit with the red glow. Nickie ventured toward the source, a gaping fissure in the rock of the cavern floor. She peered over the edge at the river of magma churning sluggishly below.

Well, shit.

That's one way to put it.

She stepped back and scratched her head, fazed by the enormity of the challenge. If she had been here alone on this mission, the problem would be nonexistent. In fact, she probably would have been wrapping this up around about now and getting the hell out of there.

This was the downside to working with other people—the lost time spent holding their hands to help them keep up. A part of her was wistful for the days when she could lone-wolf her way through whatever situation she found herself in.

Only for a moment. She remembered that she'd also had no one to laugh with and no one to light the dark along the way. A little handholding might be a fair exchange for that.

"Wait up," Grim called as he and the others entered the cavern.

"I wasn't going anywhere," she shot back. She leaned against a boulder while the others got their bearings.

John gazed around the cavern in wonder. "Wow, this place is huge. I wonder what the test is."

Nickie pointed at the tear in the rock. "I'd say the impasse we're at qualifies as a test. One that not just anyone can pass."

Grim glanced over the edge, then took a quick step back and gulped. "I'm doubting my ability to pass the test right now. That's a big fall."

"It's okay. The lava would kill you before the fall could."

Grim freaked out at that. "It doesn't matter how I would die, only that I have to get over...*that*." He pointed at the crevasse.

Adelaide came over and patted his arm. "It's okay. We can do this." She shielded her eyes from the glow and strained to see the other side of the fissure. "I can't see a way across. Looks like we'll have to make our own."

Nickie squinted, judging the distance. "I'm pretty sure I can make it across. I just don't know how to get the rest of you over there."

John shucked off his pack and began to rummage around inside. "We don't need to make a way. Here." He produced a thick coil of synthetic-looking rope, which was secured to the end of itself with a clip, so it didn't unravel. He handed the rope to Nickie, along with a mesh bag that contained the bolts to fix the line to the rock when she got across.

Adelaide eyed the rope skeptically. "How are we going to get across using just a rope?"

John stuck his hand in his pack again and came out with a zip line harness. "Easy, I thought of every eventuality."

Nickie hooked the rope over her body and walked to the edge of the tear to look for a suitable landing spot. There was a protrusion in the cliff opposite that looked wide enough to take them if they crossed one at a time and took care when they landed.

She backed up and prepared herself to take a running jump.

"Be careful!" Adelaide cried, shattering Nickie's focus.

Nickie ground to a halt before reaching the edge. "No distractions," she told Adelaide. She returned to the same spot and started again, this time without interruption. She landed on the opposite side of the crevasse with a jarring crunch and a flood of relief. She shook off the shock to her joints and got to work securing the line to the cliff wall.

She gave the line a tug when she was done, and it went taut. A couple of minutes later it dipped, and then Adelaide came flying toward her on the improvised zip line with her legs pedaling frantically in the air.

Adelaide landed awkwardly just as Nickie got out of the way. She let out a little screech as she ran to a stop before she hit the wall.

"You okay?" Nickie asked.

"Yeah, I'm good. Keen's next." Adelaide removed herself

from the harness and brushed herself down to remove the dust she'd raised with her landing.

Nickie hooked the harness back onto the rope and John pulled it back across. Keen got into the harness and paused on the edge to talk to Grim. He pushed off and landed neatly beside Nickie and Adelaide a moment later.

"What's going on over there?"

Keen wriggled out of the harness and handed it to Nickie. "Grim is asking to be left behind."

Nickie sighed. She'd had a feeling he would refuse to cross. She turned to Adelaide. "Stay here. I'll be back." She grabbed the rope with both hands and jumped to wrap her legs over it. Suspended upside-down, she pulled herself hand over hand to shinny back to the other side.

When she got there, she took the hand John offered and clambered back onto solid ground as another tremor shook the cavern.

Nickie handed the harness to John. "Just get over there. I'll take care of Grim."

John looked skeptical, but he pulled the harness on and clipped it onto the rope. "Are you sure?"

Grim's embarrassment was evident. "I'm sorry, Nickie. I just can't do it. Just leave me here. There isn't time."

As if to prove his point, the volcano gave a protracted rumble that shook the cavern and caused a layer of dust to rain down on them.

John looked up and pointed to a crack that had opened in the cavern above them. "It's too dangerous to stay here on your own. That was why I needed someone like Nickie in the first place."

"Then I'll turn back. I can get Durq and Meredith to pick me up."

"I'm not leaving you," she snapped. "What if something happens to you? No, you're crossing, Grim. We'll find a way."

John made his way to the edge and prepared to zip across. His face fell as he risked a glance down at the slowly rising magma. "Whatever you're going to do, make a decision and do it fast. This place is about to get a lot hotter."

Nickie waved him off. "Then go, and send the harness back for Grim."

John nodded and was gone.

CHAPTER 16 NICKIE

On the opposite side, Adelaide, John, and Keen did their best to work out what was going on with Grim. Nickie was gesticulating angrily, which was nothing new, and Grim was backing farther away from the edge with each second that passed.

"Do you think he'll do it?" Adelaide wondered.

Keen nodded. "He will."

John smirked. "And if he doesn't, I'm pretty sure Nickie will just fling him over her shoulder and carry him across."

Adelaide giggled. "You silly man. She's strong, but she's not *that* strong."

John gave her a knowing look. "If you think that, you're sorely mistaken. I know what she's capable of."

Keen shuffled, plucking at his suit uncomfortably. "It's getting hotter."

"I know," Adelaide agreed. "Thank goodness for these suits, or we'd be in deep trouble right about now."

John checked his suit's readout. "You're telling me. We should keep moving. Nickie and Grim will catch up." He found a handhold in the cliff face and began to climb to the top.

Keen glanced across the fissure. "Yeah, I think she's getting ready to do something anyway." He turned and joined Adelaide and John, huffing a little as he exerted himself to keep up with the others.

John reached the top first. He hauled himself over and twisted around to lean over and help Adelaide. When she was safely on the ground he went back to help Keen, but the older man just grimaced at him and worked his way up and over.

The three watched and waited while Nickie worked on getting Grim to overcome his fear of heights. A deep, protracted tremor shook chunks of rock loose from the already-crumbling roof of the cavern. It was followed by another more chilling rumble, one that wrapped cold fingers around their spines.

"What was that?" Adelaide asked, her face creased in worry. "It didn't feel like a tremor."

John dismissed Adelaide's fear with a wave. "Don't worry about it. It's just the volcano getting ready to erupt."

Keen snorted. "*Just*' the volcano. Priceless."

Adelaide was less than impressed with John's flippant attitude. "Remind me again why we decided to come along with you on this insane mission?"

John grinned. "Clearly it was because of my dashing good looks."

Adelaide gave him a cold look. "Nope. Not that. All I can think is that I must have had a moment of impaired judgment when I decided it would be a good idea to go adventuring."

The deep rumble sounded again.

Keen looked in the direction of the tunnels. "That sounds like it's getting closer."

"How can it be getting closer?" Adelaide asked in alarm.

"It's not," John insisted. "It's the tunnels, making it sound like it's getting closer." He went back to squinting through the rising steam to check on Nickie's and Grim's progress.

Unconvinced, Keen turned to Adelaide while John's attention was on their teammates. "Those rumblings are pretty intimidating, I must admit. I'm not so sure we should be this close to an eruption."

John wheeled around with a fevered grin. "Where's your sense of adventure, old man?"

"Old man?" Keen blustered. "Who are you calling old? Just because I don't fancy being burned to a crisp or crushed to death if this place comes down on top of us, it doesn't mean I've lost my sense of adventure."

John shrugged. "Just saying it how I see it. You have to let go of all that and learn to live in the moment."

Keen tensed. "That won't get us to our goal. We need to be careful, plan ahead, and stay safe."

Adelaide placed herself between the two men as they took a step toward each other. "Guys, please. You need to stay focused. Look," she pointed at Nickie, "she's on her way."

Nickie paced in front of Grim, her temper fraying as her concern for his safety grew with every shower of dirt and dust that fell. "Grim, you have to get your ass across that gap. The fucking roof is going to come down on us at any minute."

Grim had backed up against the rock face in an attempt to gain a sense of security. He cringed, his mandibles working fast enough that the translation software took a moment to decipher his words among the panicked klicks. "I want to. I just…can't make myself do it. I'm sorry. Please just go. I'll be fine."

Nickie stopped yelling and waving her arms and sighed. "No, Grim, I'm the one who's sorry. I know you're afraid." She began to pace and think instead of yelling in Grim's direction. "Let me see if Meredith can help."

There isn't much I can do to help, Meredith admitted.

There has to be something. She looked at Grim, who was shaking like a leaf as he regarded the steaming chasm with abject horror. *I'm not leaving him behind.*

I don't see how you're going to get him across if he is too traumatized to move. It's a pity he's too heavy for you to jump over with.

Nickie growled. "Fuck this!"

Grim looked up at her with puzzlement.

"One minute, Grimmie. We're going to get you over there if I have to sprout wings and fucking fly you across." *If I had just a bit of juice left I could make the jump with him. There has to be something we can do! He's my* friend, *Mere. I don't have so many of those that I can leave them to die. Please?*

There is a way, Meredith answered slowly.

Why do you sound like I'm going to be pissed at whatever you're about to tell me? Just spill it so we can get the fuck out of here. She dodged a chunk of rock that fell from the cavern roof.

You're going to be less than happy but you need to contain that and get moving. I have been slowly recharging your energy packs. You have approximately half a charge between the three packs. Meredith hesitated. *I can transfer the energy into one pack and it would be sufficient to make the jump. However, it has taken this long to gather even this much charge, Nickie. It might be a mistake to use it now.*

What's the worst that could happen? If you don't think this is the kind of situation that warrants using it, then I don't know what the fuck you're expecting us to get into.

Okay, say you use the energy pack now, and then you get hurt badly enough to need it. What will you do then?

Nickie grinned. *I'll suck it up and get on with it. Or I won't. It's worth the risk, Mere. Look at him. It's not even a choice. I refuse to leave him to fend for himself. Dude gets lost on the way from the cargo hold to the galley, for fuck's sake.*

If you're sure...

The volcano shook angrily.

Yeah, I'm completely fucking sure. Now activate the damn energy pack so I can get Grim out of here before we all die. And don't think I'm going to forget that you kept this from me.

I didn't imagine you would.

Meredith flipped the internal switch that activated the pack. Nickie wanted to sing, run, fight, and kick the ever-living shit out of anything that stood between her and her goal as the stored energy hit her nanocytes and fire flooded her body.

It was as though she'd been released from an invisible weight that had been slowing her down without her even knowing it existed. She'd been far too high to appreciate or even recognize it when the last energy pack had been activated in the bar, but she recognized it now.

She got to her feet, rolled her shoulders, and held out a hand to Grim. "Come on, Grim. I've got you. Let's get the hell out of here."

He looked up at her and shook his head, not understanding. "N-no, Nickie!"

"I'm going to jump you across. I'm at full power, but it won't last for long so hurry the fuck up. We need to get across before I drain the charge."

Grim extended a trembling hand and Nickie pulled him to his feet. His legs refused to hold him, but Nickie was ready for the adrenaline dump he was experiencing. She tucked her arms around her friend and hoisted him into a fireman's carry. "Are you ready?"

Grim shook in her arms. "No!"

"Tough titty," she replied with a chuckle. She adjusted his weight across her shoulders and backed up to the farthest point from the edge of the chasm.

You don't need that much run-up, Meredith told her.

What about the extra weight? Nickie argued. *Grim isn't exactly made of sweetness and light, and the top of the cliff is farther away than the ledge I sent the others to.* She set off, picking up speed as she went until she reached the edge and leaped without hesitation.

"Holy shit!" Keen exclaimed from the other side. "She's not gonna make it!"

The three of them watched Nickie take a flying leap toward them with Grim across her shoulders.

Adelaide gasped. "She… She is!"

Nickie and Grim landed in a messy heap on the ground beside them. Nickie groaned and pushed Grim off her. She saw he'd passed out and scrabbled to check on him.

Grim opened his eyes to see the four of them looking down at him. "Did we make it?" he managed weakly.

Nickie smirked and pulled him to his feet. "Does it feel like we didn't?"

Grim shuddered. "To be honest, a little bit. Thank you, Nickie."

"Don't mention it." She glanced at the shadows where the tunnels resumed and turned to John. "Lead the way."

Rebus Quadrant, Planet Zuifra, Reinek, Labyrinth of the Dead

They set off into the tunnel system once more, flashlights at the ready.

Nickie strode ahead to catch up with Grim, leaving Keen and Adelaide to walk together for a spell.

"How are you holding up?" he asked.

Adelaide shrugged. "It's not what I thought it would be. I didn't think I'd be so scared, but I'm handling it, I think." She turned her head to scrutinize him. "How about you? Is the level of danger everything you were hoping for?"

Keen grinned, his bushy eyebrows contracting to hide his eyes. "Hell, yeah! I haven't been this alive in years. You know, it reminds me of this planet I visited once..."

Adelaide giggled and hooked her arm through his as they walked. "Just how many planets *have* you visited? You're like a fun uncle who comes home from his travels. You have a story for every situation."

Keen puffed out his chest. "You know, I have no idea. Hundreds, I suppose. I was a Space Marine when I was a lad. We shipped out to wherever we were needed, and a few places we weren't."

"What was that like?" Adelaide asked.

Keen shrugged. "Exhilarating. There was a fair bit of waiting around, but then we'd see so many planets one after the other we lost track of where we were sometimes. I loved that. It's good to be back in the field again and remind myself that variety is the spice of life."

"I don't know," Adelaide admitted. "I'm not sure that a life filled with adventure is really for me."

Keen shook his head. "Should I remind you that you were the one who wanted more adventure?"

Adelaide looked ahead thoughtfully. "I may have bitten off more than I can chew."

Keen inclined his head. "That may be, but you're here now, so you might as well take what you can from the experience."

"Hmmm." Adelaide smirked at Keen. "Maybe I just needed a vacation from life on a mining colony.

Nickie slowed to match Grim's pace when she reached his side. "Hey."

Grim patted her on the shoulder. "Hey. Thanks for getting me across. You could have left me there, but I'm glad you didn't."

Nickie brushed his hand away. "As if I'd just leave you there to die, ass."

Grim chuckled. "I know that. I knew it before you did."

She snorted. "What, you're psychic now?"

"No," Grim told her, "I just know who you are underneath all the attitude."

Nickie picked up her pace a little to hide the shine that tried to spring to her eyes. "Fuck me. If I'd known we were going to talk about feelings, I'd have walked on my own."

Grim knew she was deflecting. "Nickie, it's okay. We can talk about something else. John, for instance."

Nickie spun to face Grim. "What? Why?"

"I'm just wondering why you're so hard on him." Grim shrugged. "He's been nothing but nice to you. I thought the mattress was a kind gesture."

Nickie scowled. "Maybe I should have left you."

Grim chuckled. "Maybe you should give John a break."

"I'll give him a break," she muttered as Grim fell back to talk to Adelaide. "His arm, his leg…"

"What are you mumbling about?" John asked as she caught up to him.

"Nothing." They were some distance ahead of the others since John was scouting ahead to search out their path to the center chambers. "Are we getting close?"

"We are. Hey, that was a good thing you did."

She looked at him blankly. "What? You mean not leaving Grim behind?"

He nodded.

Nickie's lip curled. "And you would have?"

"No…" John answered slowly. "But if I'm completely honest, you haven't struck me as the sentimental type so far."

Nickie supposed she should own that, but… "Grim is the closest thing to a friend I've got. Of-fucking-*course* I'm not going to leave him to die alone on some strange-ass planet. Fuck, what do you take me for? I'm a bitch, but I'm not completely heartless."

"I'm sorry." John had the good grace to blush.

Not that Nickie cared. She prodded him with a finger. "Now you, you're another matter completely."

John grinned. "That almost wasn't a threat! I really feel like we're making progress today."

Nickie smirked. "Shut it."

The group moved in close when the tunnel opened up once again. The rumbling had become a constant drone in the background, lending a sense of urgency to their journey into the depths of the volcano.

The cavern they came out in was the largest they'd seen yet. It was lit by the same red glow as the cavern with the crevasse, but the light was much stronger here. The downward slope continued, and the shale they were standing on crunched beneath their feet.

"What is this place?" Adelaide turned a slow half-circle.

Keen looked up at a familiar sound. "I knew it wasn't the damned lava!" He pointed into the steamy air between two rock formations.

Nickie followed Keen's finger but saw nothing. "I don't know what you saw, but th—" She was cut off by the air being driven from her body as a half-ton of living rock plowed into her from the side.

She got to her feet and kicked out at the thing that had struck her. "Get out of the way, all of you!" she shouted, seeing the rocks move again. It was some kind of stone monster. She narrowly avoided a swipe from its jagged hands and kicked it again to distract it from focusing on Adelaide, who had frozen and was within its grasp.

Keen and Grim lunged and grabbed Adelaide by the arms and pulled her to safety. Nickie relaxed fractionally when she saw them all duck into a crevice between one pile of rocks and another. *What have I got left in the tank, Meredith?*

Just your natural ability. I'm afraid your nanocytes used up the remaining energy to heal the damage to your joints after you made the jump with Grim. You fractured both your ankles on impact and tore multiple muscles and ligaments, and Grim broke three of your ribs when he landed on you.

Didn't feel a thing.

Yes, well. You will feel the next one, so concentrate.

Nickie didn't argue. She ducked around the monster and searched for a weak spot in its stone carapace. It left a trail of dust with its every movement, so Nickie figured its joints were the best place to start.

She drew her weapon, and her palm molded itself around her Jean Dukes Special like a lover on a hot summer night as she brought it up and fired. Rock chips sprayed as the shots impacted, but the monster failed to react.

Dammit! It doesn't feel pain.

She sidestepped and shot, then ducked the monster's arms and shot again twice with no more effect than if she'd been throwing flowers at the beast. *Meredith, how do I kill this fucking thing?*

You will have to dismantle it, Meredith advised.

Nickie danced as she shot. The rock monster lost

chunks of its body, and it still came at her to get to the others. *How? I can't get in close enough.*

She had no opportunity to test any theory Meredith may come up with.

The monster put on an unexpected burst of speed and lunged at Nickie. It grabbed her and flung her against the wall before she had a chance to break free of its grip.

She felt her shoulder come free from its socket as she impacted with the rock. The sudden shock masked the pain of her arm breaking as it twisted awkwardly underneath her, but only for a moment. She slid to the floor and lay still.

Fuck. This.

Get up, Nickie!

She opened one eye. *I don't fucking want to get up.* However, the monster had turned its angry little eyes on the others. She groaned and pushed herself up with her uninjured arm and squinted through swollen eyes at the oncoming monster. She felt for her Jean Dukes.

It was gone.

The pain in her shoulder and arm was immense, and it radiated out in burning waves that brought spots to her vision every time the wave peaked. *I need to get this shoulder back in and finish this.*

You know what to do, Meredith told her gently.

Nickie glanced at the monster, who was tearing up the rock around the crevice. They were firing to keep it back, but just like the suboptimal ammo she was carrying in her Jean Dukes, it had little to no effect.

Ready?

No, Nickie retorted. She clenched her teeth and looked

for a useable protrusion in the rock. She settled on one and walked over. *Count for me, Mere.*

Of course. One... Two... Thr—

Nickie slammed her dislocated shoulder into the rock and her scream pierced the cavern, bringing the monster's attention back to her. The cavern swam in her vision, fading almost to black and back again as her body fought the shock.

She screamed again, this time in rage as the monster swept around and charged her. She fished her drones out of her belt and flung them at the monster. *They'll work, right? They've got to be better than the ammo in my JD, no matter how fast it can fire a projectile.*

We will see. The drones can be directed with precision. A bullet cannot change trajectory mid-flight, Meredith replied. *What do you want from them?*

We need to take it down. Go for the legs.

Meredith sent the drones at the monster. It batted at the tiny spheres but missed, and then missed again when they whipped around and shot through its lower leg.

The monster finally reacted. It collapsed with a roar and Nickie dropped to her knees too, finally overwhelmed by the pain from her injuries. She spotted her Jean Dukes on the cavern floor, and a fresh wave of pain wracked her as she reached for the weapon and picked it up.

The monster dragged itself to shaky feet and hobbled toward her, infuriated by Meredith's constant bombardment with the drones but determined to end Nickie's existence.

John crept from the safety of the rocks and ran at the monster with his weapons drawn.

What the hell does he think he's going to do against it that I haven't already?

Men are like that, Meredith replied. *They get a little stupid when they fall for someone.*

Nickie groaned and dragged herself to her feet once again. *Not you, too. How about you all give me a break? This is not the time or place.*

Her natural healing ability had knitted her ribs, and she could almost make a fist again. Almost. She holstered her JD Special, having a much better idea instead. *Looks like I'm almost good to tag back in. Where are my drones?*

Awaiting instruction.

Good. Seeing as my ammo isn't good enough, I'm going to have to improvise. Concentrate the passes on its right arm. This fucker has annoyed me enough.

What's the plan?

I'm going to tear its arm off and beat it to death with the soggy end.

That's...creative.

Well, it was one of Aunt Bethany Anne's favorite threats when I was a kid. I always wondered if it could be done.

Let's find out then, shall we?

Nickie strode toward the beast on legs which threatened to betray her. John was having a battle all of his own. He dodged and jabbed at the monster with his sword.

Of course, *he brought a sword. A fucking* sword, *Meredith!*

I believe it is a ceremonial item. Look, he has his pistol as well.

Fat lot of good that's going to do him. Small wonder no one comes back from this place. She cupped her hands around her mouth and yelled, "Get out of the way, dumbass! You're blocking my drones."

The distraction almost cost John his life.

The monster swung an arm while John's attention was on Nickie and knocked him to the floor in a spray of teeth and blood which coated the inside of his faceplate.

"*Fuck!*" Nickie ran over to John's side.

Meredith, the drones!

She knelt to remove John's hood and check his pulse. It was still strong, so he was okay for now. She quickly wiped the blood away before she replaced his hood. The thought crossed her mind that he might not have made it, and an unwelcome twinge plucked at her insides. "You shouldn't have done that," she murmured as she quickly pulled his unconscious form into the cover of the rocks.

Meredith sent the drones zipping in formation at the monster's arm. It screeched as they tore straight through its body and out of the other side. The arm flopped uselessly at the monster's side as the drones separated it roughly at the shoulder joint.

Nickie smiled coldly as the monster flailed. Now she had a weak spot she could use to her advantage. She could say whatever she liked about her grandfather, but he had taught her well. Not that she was grateful or anything; she still hated him for every minute he'd taken from her in the name of training.

Nickie made her calculation and launched herself from John's side, leaping at the monster. She latched on to the injured arm and twisted as she landed with her feet in the armpit. She dug in with her feet and pulled on the arm in a move worthy of her Aunt Tabitha at her most unthinking.

The arm came free with a dry pop and Nickie fell back with the arm on top of her. She scrambled to her feet and avoided the monster's thrashing feet, using her dodge to wind up and swing for the monster's head with her improvised club. She felt her almost-healed arm break again but she was beyond caring.

The monster didn't know what had hit it. Its head snapped back and slammed against the wall, dazing it.

Nickie pushed through the burning in her muscles and the white-hot bolts of pain shooting up her rebroken arm and swung the monster's arm again and again.

The arm shattered on the seventh blow, but by then she didn't need to keep going anyway. The monster lay completely unmoving on the cavern floor, defeated. She bent over and rested her weight on her good arm while she got her breath and forced down the nausea from the pain as her arm knitted again.

John made his way out from behind the rocks and came to sit beside her. "My hero."

Nickie grinned. She undid her faceplate and gingerly explored the area around her busted eye with a fingertip. "You helped."

They leaned back against the rock and breathed through the relief of surviving the battle. Adelaide and Keen emerged from their hiding place, followed by Grim, who bitched at Keen as they made their way over to Nickie and John. "You blocked my view the entire time, I didn't see any of the fight!"

The three of them helped Nickie and John to their feet, and they headed into the next set of tunnels.

Grim paused by the rocky corpse and sighed. "No one

ever saves any of the action for me." He prodded the nose of the inert beast with a foot and hopped back half a step when the head shifted.

Grim took another step back when the monster's eye opened and fixed him with an enraged stare. He backpedaled and ran after the others before they disappeared into the narrow tunnel without him.

CHAPTER 17 NICKIE

Nickie and John supported each other as the group limped deeper into the tunnel system. The incline in this section was much sharper, leading them ever closer to the center of the volcano.

They lagged a little way behind Keen and Adelaide, and Grim was out in front of them all since he was embarrassed about haring past them when the monster woke up.

"I can't believe what a beating that thing took and lived," Nickie marveled. She rubbed her ribs, which were getting less sore by the minute. She was bone-tired, though, as her nanocytes worked at their usual capacity to heal her injuries.

"How's the arm? Three breaks is a lot for one day." John slurred a little as he spoke. He was in a slightly more difficult situation than Nickie since the blow he'd taken from the monster had cracked his cheekbone and he didn't have nanocytes rapidly repairing him.

Nickie regarded the multicolored bruise gracing his face. "My arm will be fine in a few hours. What about your face? You're gonna need some Pod-doc time to get that looking pretty again."

"You think I'm pretty?" John teased.

Nickie arched an eyebrow. "I think you were a total dumbass going after that rock beast with a fucking sword."

"Hey, don't mock the decades-old traditions of my ancestors." John winced as he grinned at his joke without thinking. "Ow, that shit hurts. But you're welcome."

Nickie bumped him with her good shoulder. "I was getting to that part. Thank you for distracting it while I set my shoulder."

John shook his head. "I still can't believe you put it back in that way. That took guts."

Nickie nodded. "I know it did. If I'd hit it wrong my shoulder would have been completely fucked. This is not my first rodeo, Prince P... John."

That brought another wince from the prince. He bent over and clutched his ribs as he shook with laughter.

"What's so funny?" Nickie demanded.

John waved his free hand. "Nothing. It's just, that's the first nice thing you've said to me since we met and you *still* almost insulted me."

Nickie? Sorry to interrupt.

Then don't.

Nice to see you've got your snark back. I've been taking seismic readings while you were off playing with rocks, and I have concluded that there will be an eruption within the next few hours.

That soon? We'd better get our asses in gear then before we get a nasty surprise.

Actually, I recommend that you turn back now. It's not safe.

What? But we're almost there! Aren't we?

You're not close enough to procure the plant and make it back to the foot of the volcano before it erupts. It would be wise to leave as soon as possible.

Hang on, I need to discuss this with the others.

She called a halt and gathered everyone in. "Meredith has told me that the volcano is going to erupt within the next few hours. She's recommending that we turn back now while we have time to make it to the surface. I'm happy to go on, but I'm not making that decision for the rest of you."

John straightened up. "I'm not going back. I have to get the plant to heal my father. I've come this far, and I'm not giving up when we're so close."

Keen's face reddened. "Did you not hear what Nickie just said? We should turn back before we get caught in the eruption."

John threw up his hands in frustration. "I won't turn back. You can all leave without me if you want, but I won't fail. It's not far now. We're near the center. I know it."

Keen clenched his fists. "That's the thing. You *don't* know it. All we've had to guide us is rumor and fable, and we've pushed our luck far enough. It's time to leave before it's too late and we *can't* leave."

John started forward. "Leave if you want to, but why did you insist on coming if you were just going to back out at the last minute?"

Keen got in John's face. "Maybe if I'd known what we were up against I would have thought twice about joining you."

"Yeah, well, maybe you're just not cut out for this kind

of thing. Maybe you should have just stayed home. Then we'd be in there getting the plant to save my father instead of standing here arguing about it with you!"

Adelaide was almost in tears. "Please don't argue! We need to stick together."

Grim got between the two men and pushed them apart. "This isn't the time to fall apart. We will decide the best course of action as a group."

John stamped his foot and pointed down the tunnel. "It's. Right. Down. *There!* How much simpler can it be? We're wasting time, and we need to move."

Nickie held up a finger. "One minute." *Meredith, how close are we to our goal?*

John is almost correct. My scans indicate a large chamber at the end of this tunnel. It is likely the one that contains the plant you are searching for.

She turned her attention back to the others. "Meredith says there's a chamber at the end of this tunnel. I think we should split up. John and I will retrieve the plant, you three make your way back to the ship."

Grim interrupted, "You want us to leave without you? I don't like that as a plan."

It may be a problem, Meredith agreed. *The magma levels have begun to rise, and the zip line will not be there when you return.*

Nickie relayed the information to the others. "So you don't need to worry about making the crossing."

Grim's concern deepened. "But we will also need to find an alternative way out. It's better if we stick together."

"Fuck it all, you're right." Nickie looked at Adelaide and Keen. "What's it going to be? Will you see this through?"

They exchanged a glance, and Adelaide squared her shoulders determinedly. "I'm in."

Keen sighed wearily. "I suppose I am, too."

Nickie turned to Grim. "What about you, Grim?"

Grim opened his arms wide and made a little bow. "I but follow wherever you lead." He straightened and set off walking. "Just be sure to lead us out, okay?"

Nickie grinned. "Well, shit. Looks like we're doing this."

The tension increased incrementally with the temperature as they got ever closer to the center of the volcano. The tunnel was littered with fallen rocks, forcing them to walk single-file and work their way around the piles as they went.

Nickie hung back a little while she and Meredith plotted their route out. The others pressed on with the ever-present rumble of the impending eruption growing louder in their ears the farther along the tunnel they progressed.

John led them at a brisk pace, his desire to get to the chamber overwhelming the need for safety.

Grim and Adelaide picked their way along in his wake, chatting as they clambered over and around the rockfalls.

Grim caught Adelaide when she slipped on a patch of lichen. He helped her right herself and spotted the ashen cast to her face. "Hey, are you okay?"

Adelaide nodded and carried on down the tunnel. "Thanks, I'm fine. A little scared still, is all. I figure that the center is the most dangerous place to be, and we're heading right for it."

Grim nodded. "I get that. It can be difficult to face your fears, but sometimes we have to face the thing we fear the most to escape the prison we allowed it to create for us."

Adelaide gazed at Grim in full awe. "How did you get so wise, Grim?"

Grim sniggered. "I don't know about that. You just have to learn from your experiences."

Adelaide looked thoughtful. "Then you must have had a lot of experiences."

John called from up ahead. "I can see the end of the tunnel. We made it!"

They caught up with him, and they entered the chamber as a group. The tunnel opened up onto a wide, sloping plateau that ended in a drop-off at an aperture a short distance away. The chasm looked to stretch all the way around the chamber, although much of it was obscured from their position by huge rockpiles and odd-looking magma sculptures.

"We need to get to the other side," John told them. He fished a pair of binoculars from his pack. "I'm going to look for a way across."

"Good idea," Nickie agreed. "We should all look. This place is huge, and time is short. Split up for now, but don't go too far. Everyone meet back here in ten minutes."

Keen and Adelaide went one way, Grim went another.

Nickie scanned the chamber around her but she didn't see any plants, just solidified magma and steam rising up out of the ground everywhere she looked. "Looks like this place has seen some serious activity." She walked over to where John stood peering over the edge of the precipice at the magma below through his binoculars.

He turned his head to look at Nickie, his face glistening with sweat in the dull glow of the magma. "It's rising," he informed her.

Nickie chose a spot on the opposite wall just above the lava-line and kept her eyes on it. A couple of minutes later the spot was overtaken by the magma. "I can see that." She strained her eyes to try and make out what was on the other side. The ground rose in hissing mounds where the pressure from below had forced it up in tiny versions of the mountain. The natural vents hissed continuously, superheating the air inside the chamber. "That looks like vegetation over there," she told John, pointing out one of the dark patches. "Are any of those your plant?"

John trained his binoculars on the vents. "I think... Yes, I can see it! We just need to get over there."

"Here, let me see." Nickie held out her hand, and John passed her the binoculars. She used them to scan the edge of the aperture and saw Grim waving at her from his position on top of a jutting outcrop. She turned to John. "Go and get Adelaide and Keen. It looks like Grim's found us a place to cross."

Nickie made her way to Grim over the treacherous ground and looked across the aperture. The outcrop extended almost to the center of the chasm, where it broke off and then resumed from the other side. "It almost looks like a bridge."

Grim tilted his head as he examined the narrow bridge. "I think it looks like two fingertips almost touching."

Nickie grinned. "You romantic bastard. Come on, let's get across."

Nickie, that promontory will not hold Grim. It is extremely porous.

"Oh." She grabbed Grim by the arm before he could take a step onto the crumbling bridge. "Meredith says it won't hold your weight. Sorry, dude, you're benched for this one."

Grim huffed. "If I keep getting left out, then I don't know if I'll bother coming along on the next mission."

Nickie shrugged. "I'm sure you'll get some action, just not now." She indicated the slowly creeping magma below. "Unless you really want a lava bath?"

Nickie was cut off when the background rumble suddenly increased to a roar, and the ground rippled beneath their feet and threw her off-balance. She pitched forward into the nearest rockpile. Without a thought, she put out the arm she'd broken earlier to save herself. It buckled, and she slammed into the rock face-first with a scream of agony as the bone in her arm parted yet again. "*Fuck!*"

Grim helped her up when the contraction had passed. "Are you okay?"

They had to almost yell to be heard above the grinding complaints of the volcano. "I'm fine. It's just a cut."

She held a hand to her head, probing gently through her hood. Her busted eye had opened up in a ragged gash where she'd scraped her face. She wiped the blood away and turned back to the bridge. "Shit, more of the bridge has fallen away." The cavern swam in her vision, and Grim caught her again as she stumbled. "Maybe I banged my head a bit harder than I thought."

Your ulna has rebroken, and you have the beginnings of a concussion. You need to take it easy while your brain heals.

Yeah, 'cuz there's plenty of opportunities to kick back and relax right now, Mere.

Whatever you are doing, you need to hurry. That was a massive spike in the seismic activity since my last report. Get the plant and get the hell out of there, Nickie.

Keen and Adelaide arrived at a jog. Keen took one look at the bridge and began to shake his head emphatically. "There's no way we can cross that."

Nickie waved him off and tottered toward the bridge. "We can, and we will. Where's John?"

Adelaide frowned. "I thought he was with you and Grim?"

"No, or I wouldn't be asking. Didn't you pass him on your way here?" She turned in the direction of the last place she'd seen him. "You all wait here, and I'll find him. Try to figure out how we can get across that bridge without dying while I'm gone, okay?"

Nickie set off without waiting for a reply. John was not at the spot she'd left him. She called his name, but there was no way he'd hear her over the growing roar of the volcano. She looked around and spotted his binoculars on the ground, then saw his foot protruding from behind a boulder.

She hurried over and found him propped up against the rock with his head in his hands. "John, what's going on?"

He looked up at her with confusion. "Nickie? I climbed up to get a better view and slipped."

She held out her hand. "Come on, we've found a way across."

He pointed at his foot, which was at an awkward angle to his leg. "It's broken."

Nickie sighed. "No shit. Can you get up?"

John struggled to his feet, and she wrapped an arm around him to support him as they walked back to the bridge.

The others were still debating the options when Nickie guided John over to sit against a rock. "What's the problem?"

Keen's face was the reddest Nickie had seen it. "This is suicidal! That bridge won't hold any of us." He pointed at Nickie and John. "You're both too damn injured to be of any use, and the fucking thing will collapse if either Grim or I even attempt to cross."

Grim nodded in agreement. "We might have to just call it quits, Nickie. We can't win every one."

Nickie bristled. "I don't quit." She laughed as her vision swam again. "Okay, I don't quit anymore. The point is that I'm not leaving without that plant to save John's dad." She took a wobbly step toward the bridge.

"I can do it." Adelaide's voice was a whisper in the thunder of the cavern.

Nickie heard, and she eyed Adelaide suspiciously. "I suppose you're light enough to get over without the bridge collapsing, but you haven't got training for this. How will you cross the gap?"

Adelaide shook her head to dislodge the strand of sweaty hair from her face and half-shrugged. "I have some gymnastics skills. Same thing." She turned and ran toward the bridge. "Just watch!"

She vaulted up onto the rocks and gained the bridge. "See?" she called back. She hurried over the wider part but slowed as the rock narrowed closer to the middle before ending abruptly. Adelaide brought her arms out for balance as she placed her feet carefully to avoid falling to her death.

Back on the far side, Nickie stayed by John and held her breath as she watched Adelaide's progression. Keen and Grim called encouragement from the edge to keep Adelaide's confidence high while she climbed around the rubble in her way.

The bridge narrowed to just a few paces wide. Adelaide halted. "Guys?" She looked back at them, her face completely drained of color. "I don't know. I can make the jump, but what if it doesn't hold me?"

The bridge shook minutely, and Adelaide almost lost her footing. "I'm going to try." She backed up a few paces, sprinted at the gap, and vaulted over to the other side.

She landed at a run and pelted toward the vegetation around the vents without stopping.

Nickie came over to stand with Grim and Keen. She handed over John's binoculars wordlessly while Adelaide swerved around the continuous jets of steam the vents on the other side were emitting.

A few tense minutes later, Adelaide returned to the bridge and gave them a thumbs up.

Grim turned and called to John, "She has the plant."

John nodded and slumped against the rock. They

shared a relieved grin as Adelaide made her way back to them.

Their relief was short-lived.

As Adelaide reached top speed to jump the gap, a keening roar came from the tunnel behind them. Adelaide lost her footing on the jump, and she screamed as she missed her landing.

Nickie moved like the wind to reach her, pushing through the dizziness that washed over her from the sudden movement.

Nickie, no!

Nickie didn't listen. The bridge crumbled with every panicked step she took. She dropped to her stomach as the dizziness returned and inched her way along until she reached the edge and found Adelaide hanging on grimly to the rock. She reached out with her good arm as Adelaide cried with relief. "Take my hand!"

She grabbed Nickie's hand, and Nickie slid backward on her stomach to pull her up one agonizing inch at a time.

Adelaide sobbed as they crawled to safety. "Thank you! Thank you!"

"Don't thank me, just hurry up before the fucking monster gets here and cuts off our escape." She grabbed Adelaide and pulled her along, the dizziness threatening to overwhelm her completely.

They clung to each other for support as they reached the other side. When they reached solid ground, Adelaide collapsed to her knees and let the tears flow. She undid the pouch on her suit and passed the plants she had stuffed inside to John.

John's eyes shone. "Thank you. I can't tell you what this

means to me…"

Another roar came from the tunnel, and the cavern vibrated as the monster approached.

Nickie turned tiredly toward the tunnel. "Nope, you can't. We haven't got time." *Meredith, get us out of here now!*

The route map is ready, but you need to hurry. There is another activity spike, this one ten times any of my previous readings. The eruption has begun. Take the path I'm overlaying in your HUD. It will lead you to an exit partway up the volcano from which you can escape.

A blue line appeared over Nickie's vision just as the monster appeared. "Grim, take John, and everyone follow me. We're getting the fuck out of here."

Grim hoisted John over his shoulder and ran after Nickie as if his life depended on it.

Even inside their suits, the heat was becoming unbearable as the magma overflowed the aperture. The monster paid it no attention, too focused on the group to notice its encroaching death. They dodged behind the rocks to stay out of its line of sight, but it still came after them, screeching as it smashed the rockpiles with its remaining arm.

They ran.

A rockpile exploded right next to the monster, and a jet of lava spewed out. The pressure knocked the monster into the aperture, ending it forever and ticking one item off Nickie's "things to worry about" list.

Nickie led them along the route Meredith had given her, screaming encouragement at them as they went. One of the vents exploded in a hail of shrapnel that only just missed Keen and Adelaide.

Nickie looked back and saw they'd slowed. "Do not stop putting one foot in front of the other until we are safe and sound, do you hear me? Now fucking run! There's the tunnel."

They picked up the pace again once they'd squeezed into the tunnel. It shook around them, the walls and roof showering them with ash and dust. It twisted and turned, and they ran in labored silence for what felt like eons as the volcano shook itself to pieces around them.

As they neared the exit, the rising magma began to gain speed. The imminent eruption was no longer imminent.

Nickie's enhanced vision picked up the increase in the light level just before they rounded another bend and found themselves in a large cave.

Adelaide cheered exhaustedly. "We made it!"

Nickie took a moment to check everyone over. Grim was clearly running on empty but still carried John resolutely. Keen leaned on a rock and heaved in grateful lungfuls of air, but appeared to be fine otherwise. She glanced back at the tunnel they'd just left and saw the familiar dull glow of the approaching magma. She pointed to the tunnel. "We haven't made it yet. Let's go."

Nickie recognized their location as soon as they stepped outside of the cave and she saw the bare rock below. They'd dismissed this cave as an entry point since it would have been a bitch to ascend the smooth slope.

However, as an emergency exit, it couldn't have been more ideal.

"Just like a slide," Keen chuckled. "Only if we get stuck on this one, we die."

"Best get going then," Nickie replied.

CHAPTER 18 NICKIE

Rebus Quadrant, Planet Zuifra, Reinek, Outside the Volcano

They began the descent, doing what they could to stay in control of their speed. Gravity and the urgency of the approaching lava flow won out, and they arrived at the bottom of the volcano in tangled heaps of bruised and battered limbs.

The group scrambled to their feet as the biggest rumble yet shook the ground beneath them, and a dark cloud appeared at the edge of the caldera.

Nickie didn't give anyone a chance to freeze up. "Grab each other and run!"

The pyroclastic cloud spilled down the volcano toward them, and they raced for their lives once again. The boiling ash began to pick up speed, and Nickie didn't know if they were going to make it. Visibility was down to nothing, and all she could hope was that they could all hold on until they reached the ship.

The blue line in her HUD cut out suddenly. *Meredith, where is our exit?*

Look up.

Nickie shielded her eyes against the hot ash rain and saw the *Penitent Granddaughter* coming in to land. *Thank fuck for that.* She let out a long, slow breath as the relief of seeing her ship set in.

The others were just as happy to see Durq open the ramp to let them in. The ramp stirred the ash as it landed with a soft thump and they all piled onboard. As the ramp began to close behind them Grim's legs finally gave way, and he lowered John to the deck

Keen came over to help John, who stumbled on his broken ankle and fell backward toward the door. Keen grabbed him and pulled him back, then stumbled from exhaustion himself as he took the other man's weight.

John hung onto Keen to steady himself and they laughed as they hugged and backslapped. "Appreciate the assist, man."

"Any time," Keen replied. "But you know you owe me now, right?"

They laughed again and set off for the med bay, using each other as crutches.

Nickie sat on a crate getting her breath back when Durq almost knocked the wind out of her again with a bearhug. He released her and nodded without making eye contact. "Glad you're okay."

Nickie got up, and for the first time, the little Skaine didn't flinch away from her. She grinned and gathered him in a return hug. "I'm happy to see you, too."

· · ·

Rebus Quadrant, Aboard the *Penitent Granddaughter*, Mess

Nickie sat back in her chair, already feeling half-healed.

The Yollin whiskey probably had a lot to do with it, although having good company to share in the victory was actually pretty sweet as well.

They were all clean, fed, and rested, and the meal Grim had prepared, as well as the amount of alcohol they had washed it down with, had left them relaxed and companionable. Keen and Grim were up to their usual pastime of competitive story-telling for the group's entertainment.

Nickie sipped her whiskey and smiled at Grim's recounting of how Keen had shoved him into the crevice and blocked his view of Nickie's fight with the rock monster. "What about you, Adelaide?"

Adelaide looked at Nickie with the eyes of a woman who'd had a long day and just a smidge too much to drink. "Huh?"

"What made you step up like that at the bridge?"

Adelaide's eyes widened in comprehension. "Oh, that! I just decided to take Grim's advice. Life's too short to quit when it gets hard. I had value on this mission I hadn't expected to."

John clapped in agreement. "Well said! So, what happened on the other side of the bridge? I couldn't see a thing from where I was."

Adelaide gasped. "It was the strangest place! Like…" She sniggered as it came to her. "Like another planet! I couldn't see a thing above my waist once I headed into the steam, and it was too hot to stand anyway so I had to crawl along until I found the plants. I just grabbed them and got the hell out of there."

Grim turned to John. "Will your father be okay now?"

John nodded. "He will, and I couldn't have done it without all of you." He raised his glass. "A toast to teamwork!"

They all joined the toast, and the storytelling resumed. Keen launched into an anecdote that required a lot of space to tell. Grim, Adelaide, and Durq moved to the end of the table to get a better viewing position, leaving Nickie and John to chat at the quieter end.

John sat next to Nickie, picking at the remainder of his food. He pushed his plate away when Nickie upended the last of the whiskey into their glasses. Half his face was obscured by a large dressing over the broken cheekbone he'd gotten fighting the monster, and he sat slightly twisted to keep his broken ankle elevated on the chair between them.

Nickie nodded at his plaster cast. "Bet that didn't go as easily as my shoulder."

John chuckled. "That's putting it lightly. I meant what I said about teamwork. I really couldn't have succeeded without you." He ran his finger through the puddle of condensation caused by his glass. "That's what I learned from this. It's okay to lean on others when you need help. I thought I understood that when I decided to come looking for you, but I didn't. Not really."

Nickie glanced over at the others as they burst out laughing again. "I think you're right. They've gotten under my skin, whether I like it or not. I'm trying not to push them away because I care." She broke off while she dealt with the lump forming in her chest. "I just don't know why it has to be so damn hard to trust people."

John looked at her thoughtfully. "You must trust me to tell me this."

She looked away. "You're just easy to talk to. Anyway, it's not like you're sticking around, so...whatever." She got up and drained her glass. "I'm gonna call it a night, get some sleep before we get back to the colony. You want a hand getting back to your quarters?"

John smiled. "That would be great, thanks."

She hooked his arm over her shoulder and waved to the others.

"Night!" Adelaide called cheerily.

Keen continued his story as they left the mess and headed down the corridor toward the sleeping quarters, laughing and joking until they reached John's door.

Nickie shrugged his arm off and stepped back to give him space to get to the door. The alcohol she'd consumed had left her feeling contemplative, and his comment about trust hit home. As he turned to say goodnight, she gave in and stopped denying herself the chance of a connection. "You could stay with me tonight."

John's dimple appeared at the edge of his dressing. He took her hand. "I could... And I want to. But no."

Nickie frowned. "Why, if you want to?"

He grinned. "Because I just watched you make the decision. I want you to think on it for a while first, okay?" He leaned in and kissed the corner of her mouth. "But when you're ready..." He stepped inside his quarters and closed the door.

Nickie stood there for a moment, totally unable to

process what had just happened. She regained her composure and continued to her quarters. She got inside and leaned on the door after she'd closed it behind her. *Meredith?*

Yes?

What the fuck just happened?

I don't know what you mean, Nickie.

I mean, is John really for real? She stared at her empty bed. *Most guys would have taken the wild night and been done. Fuck, why did he have to be one of the respectful ones?*

You don't want to be respected?

I think a certain amount of healthy fear is okay, but this scares the shit out of me. What do I do with a good guy? What if I break him or something? She changed into a t-shirt and climbed into bed. A thought slipped across her consciousness as she passed into sleep.

What if he changes me?

Rebus Quadrant, Themis Colony, Mess Hall

Nickie felt a little bit like she'd come home. She was surrounded by people she knew and didn't hate. People who had been glad to see her return. That had surprised the hell out of her since she hadn't gone to any great lengths to fit in. Her actions had apparently spoken for her, however, because the colonists had welcomed her back yesterday with open arms.

The continuing improvement in the colony's quality of life now they had the food situation in hand was a big deal to them, and last night she'd been dragged up on stage by

Raynard, along with the other workers, to celebrate the success of the biomes.

The vibrant atmosphere was the same this morning in the bustling mess hall as people hurried through breakfast to begin their day's work. It warmed Nickie to see the confidence returning to the colony, and it was also satisfying to know she'd had a hand in hope returning.

John stood up with his breakfast tray. "Will you all come to see me off?"

There was a round of yesses from everyone around the table, but John's eyes rested on Nickie as he spoke. "Great. I'll be leaving as soon as my pre-flight checks are done. I have to get this plant back to my father."

They gathered at the airfield a short time later to say their goodbyes. John went to each of them to give them his thanks for their part in his success.

Keen slapped John on the back and laughed loudly. "You know, we made quite the team out there."

John grinned and returned the gesture. "That we did. But I have to get back with the plant and claim my place as future leader." He hugged Nickie tightly. "When I'm done back home, I'm heading out of this quadrant. Maybe I'll see you around sometime?"

Nickie tilted her head. "You're going back to the Federation? Then no."

John grinned his easy grin. "Nuh-uh, the other way."

Nickie frowned. "But there's nothing out there."

He winked at her as he entered the *Briar Rose*. "That's what we want you to think."

The door to the ship closed behind him, leaving Nickie

standing on the airstrip with her mouth opening and closing in indignation.

"You ok?" Adelaide asked.

Nickie growled and stalked toward the *Penitent Granddaughter*. "That *man!*" She stopped and looked back at the others. "Well, are you coming? Ship can't leave without its crew."

CHAPTER 19 NICKIE

Rebus Quadrant, Aboard the *Penitent Granddaughter*, Bridge

The ship lifted into the atmosphere. The mood on the bridge was one of celebration and excitement for the new beginning they had grasped. When they were well underway, everyone undid their harnesses and began talking about where they would go next.

Nickie watched them from her customary position in the captain's chair with her feet crossed on the console. These were her crew. Hers. She settled in.

Durq flitted from person to person, never staying for more than a snatch of conversation. Nickie saw the improvement in his confidence, though.

She remembered the quivering mess he'd been when she'd rescued him from being his former shipmates' dinner and grinned at the sight of his creepy-ass smile, which now that she'd seen it a few times wasn't so creepy anymore.

Keen pottered around after Grim, who was gratefully showing him the ropes and enthusing about being able to devote himself to his art. Adelaide stayed at her console, already deep into the *Granddaughter's* technical manuals.

Nickie hadn't experienced this before. Sure, she'd lived alongside it, but she'd always held herself aloof, never fully immersing herself in the concept of belonging. She had come to the conclusion long ago that she would rather be alone, but now she realized that she wanted something more than solitude.

She knew she still had a hell of a long way to go, but she didn't feel the maybe anymore. She felt the tiny beginning of hope.

It is good to see you this close to contentment.

Nickie broke from her reverie at Meredith's interruption. *I guess I do feel pretty good about things.*

Will this good feeling extend to sharing your space over a longer period of time?

Nickie considered the question for a long moment. *I don't know. Before I would have said they all come with too much baggage, physical and emotional. I would have run screaming from it. Now...it doesn't seem like such a big deal if someone leaves their gear lying around or wants to talk about their day.*

And what about the prince?

Nickie's mouth twitched. *Him? He's a pain in my ass already. I kind of like it, though. I want to know what he was being all mysterious about before he left.*

She got up out of her chair to speak. "Okay, crew, it's time to stop the chin-wagging and get on with finding our next adventure."

Keen stood to attention. "What are your orders, Captain?"

Nickie sat down again. "Oh. Um, I haven't gotten that far yet. Before John left, he said something about heading away from his homeworld. In the opposite direction from the Federation."

Keen's frown mirrored Nickie's earlier confusion. "But there's nothing *in* that direction. Just empty space."

Nickie shrugged. "That's what I thought, but John hinted differently. I can't resist a mystery."

Meredith joined in via the speaker. "I have scanned in that direction, but this Skaine technology is not picking anything up."

Nickie waved a hand. "See? It's fucking odd. There must be something out there. So, orders...wanna go and poke around and see what we find out there?"

Keen hurried to his seat and began strapping in. "Yes, Captain!"

"Yes, ma'am!" Adelaide chirped.

Durq clapped with excitement.

"Permission to whoop?" Grim asked.

Nickie grinned. "Permission granted. Set a course for the mystery, Meredith."

"Already done," Meredith replied. "I'm just awaiting the order."

Nickie put her feet back up on the console and twirled a finger. "Make it so."

Unknown Location

The purloined message on the screen was paused on John Deblanc's earnest face. It was a lucky intercept, caught by chance. It could be nothing, but it could also be exactly what he'd been searching for.

He played it to be certain before he notified anyone else:

"Hi, Mom, Dad. Sorry I kinda disappeared for a while there. I didn't mean to worry you so much that you sent someone after me."

John appeared suitably abashed for a moment, then he grinned and held up a bunch of plants with their roots wrapped in cloth to the camera. His message continued:

"The legends were true, and I made it through the volcano alive. I have the cure for Dad!" He stashed the plants and faced the screen again. "I have so much to tell you both, but I know you'll want to hear this first. I went to find the woman you sent to come help me. You must have known I'd find out. Anyway, did you know that you sent an actual Grimes after me? Anyway, I'm on my way home now, and I'll tell you both all about Nickie and her crew when I get there. Love you both."

The video ended and the young prince's face froze on the happy-go-lucky grin once again.

The message remained paused.

A few moments later there was a knock on the door of the office.

"Come in," the viewer of the message called.

The door opened, and a woman strode in and perched on his desk. "Hey, what's up?" She glanced at the tablet on his desk. "Ooh, who's the cutie?"

He slid the tablet over to her. "Prepare yourself."

She frowned and took the tablet. "What is it?"

"Just watch."

She pressed Play and watched the short message in silence.

Then she watched again, and again.

She was about to play it a fourth time when the tablet was tugged gently from her hands. She looked up with tears tracking down her cheeks. "Does this mean…"

Barnabas nodded. "Yes, Tabitha. She is beginning to heal."

FINIS

AUTHOR NOTES - ELL LEIGH CLARKE

WRITTEN AUGUST 12, 2018

Thank yous!

As always massive thanks goes out to MA for working on this project with me... even while he's gallivanting across half the continent... and otherwise. (He's probably already told you he was in Asia for a few weeks this month!).

Don't worry, chap. We held the fort while you were gone... and while there is video footage of Jeff and I pulling your leg in your absence while we worked on the covers, it's only going up on Patreon... so you won't see it!

Bwhahahahahahah :D

JIT and Steve

Huge gratitude bombs going out to our dedicated and relentless JITers. Without you we'd be making boobs of ourselves will silly errors. Thanks for catching them. And for the positive feedback. You have no idea how helpful it is to know that we're on the right track! You're the best.

Thanks also to Zen Master Steve. Goodness knows

how he manages to do all he does... and keep a cool head... but it's super appreciated. Thanks Steve :)

(Ooops. Microsoft put a fancy emoticon in there. I've fixed it. Text only! I got it!)

Aside: Last book Steve ended up having to reupload the book after going through and taking out a bunch of emoticons in the author notes. Apparently, MA and I are the worst.

It makes me wonder if we should be more expressive with our language... rather than resorting to the short hand of millennials. Perhaps that's something to consider. After all, we do put "writer" on our tax returns. I think with that identity we might need to embrace some form of writerly responsibility. Or at least word-smithery.

I will try harder.

Reviewers

I'd love to extend a HUGE thank you to our amazing Amazon reviewers. It's because of you that we get to do this full time. Without your five-star reviews and thoughtful words on Amazon we simply wouldn't have enough folks reading these space shenanigans to be able to write full time.

You are the reason these stories exist. So, truly, thank you.

Readers and FB page supporters

Last, and certainly by no means least, I'd like to thank you for reading this book... and all the others. Your enthusiasm for the world, and the characters, is heart-warming. Your words of encouragement, and demands for the next episode, are the things that keep us going through the looooong hours of writing, punching and plotting.

Thank you for being here, for reading, for reviewing, and for always brightening my day with your words of support on the fb and Patreon pages.

Thank you.

E x

Solo Deuces

This episode was particularly tricky to write, partly because MA was 'out of pocket' for most of the time of writing. Not only that, and this may come as a complete shock to you, but I'm writing this having finished punching the Nickie side of the story and still not seen anything about Tabitha.

I mean, sure, we had *a* story meeting about the larger theme and what Tabby needed to accomplish... but details? Beats? Words? Nada! So, as I'm writing this, I hope it works.

I mean, I think it has in the past. To be fair we had practice at this with the last two Dark Ages books. But as I'm typing my scrivener file is open and where the Tabitha scenes will go I have place holders saying: "Tabitha".

Fingers crossed he gets it to me before Steve needs the file for Editing and JIT! ;)

MA says Tabitha, I say Nickie

Explain that when I label my files, coz I write the Nickie part. Sometimes forget, and get confused when MA sends me Tabitha stuff.

Of course, he gives me grief for this, proclaiming it to be a Tabitha book…

MA and "You're right"

You're right isn't something that MA says willingly or often.

It normally involves tonnes of reasoning (which is mostly futile) and waiting for him to emotionally come around to a different way of thinking. It happens. But it can take anything from a few minutes (of tantrum or push back) to *several* months of just not mentioning it.

It's often worth the wait.

The other day he called me from China while I was having a lie down. (The recovery from adrenal failure is still progressing well, but I can't keep going all day yet). He asked about some of the words we'd been working on and I told him I had a problem with some of the sentence structures so I was punching them.

It was a minor point.

But… whether it was because he'd just woken up, or because he was taking it personally, he insisted on seeing what I was doing.

Ellie: dude, we've done like 16 books together? Surely at this point you can trust my judgement.

MA: no. it's not that. And the logic doesn't follow.

Ellie: how come?

MA: because in those 16 books I wasn't reading for this.

Ellie: and? It clearly wasn't something you wanted switching back. And besides, clearly you trust my judgement in order to write that many books with me. And can I just say: Dark Ages?

MA: waffle waffle.

Ellie: So I'm right?

MA: waffle waffle. A few moments of randomness go past.

Ok. Yes. You're right. Ok. Fine.

(beat)

MA: Shut up.

MA and business decisions

Later in the same conversation we were talking about some business-y stuff. I was gently asking questions to figure out what his motivations were... and giving an alternative viewpoint on stuff he may or may not have considered already.

He sounded grumpy, so I thought I'd try and smooth it over.

Ellie: hey, look, I'm the only one who will say these things to you. So do you want me to stop?

MA: waffle waffle. No.

Ellie: coz I can stop. And then... you can just do whatever you want, in total peace.

MA: waffle waffle.

Ellie: But you know I'm right. And you'd-

MA: yes. You're right. Ok? Do you want to get it on a recording?

Ellie: no. It's ok. It's more important that you understand that I'm right, than I hear it!

MA: Hahahaha. (beat) Shut up.

I know. He's got a tough job.

But at least he can admit it when someone else is probably right. Well done, Yoda. Well done. :)

Labor Day

If you're a long-term reader of my little corner of the Kurtherian Universe you'll already be aware that I moved to the US about a year and a bit ago. I spent my first year in LA and then at the beginning of this year moved to Austin, Texas.

And this will be the first year that I'll be celebrating Labor Day like a native.

Woot!

It's all thanks to Amy.

Amy is one of my writer friends. She hangs out at my place quite a bit. You may have seen pictures of us going to see movies or hanging out in the local café. Anyway, we've started watching old movies (that we feel we ought to have seen before) at my place, using a projector set up. (Coz projectors, like bow-ties, are cool! – you should excuse the Doctor Who reference if you're not familiar with the show.)

When we watch movies at the theatre there are strict no talking rules - under pain of death from Shelia the Velociraptor.

https://www.youtube.com/watch?v=1K9g18kEx-0

At my place there are no such rules.

Or velociraptors.

And so, we stop the movie every so often when we want to talk. It's a hoot. And we discuss everything from the profound to the ridiculous.

My writing about this in the last author notes led Amy to suggest that we should probably do this on a live stream. So that's what we're going to do. It's open to all levels in Patreon, and we're even taking a vote on which movie you want us to watch. You can even watch the movie along with us. In fact, I'd recommend that, because then you'll see what we're talking about.

It's going to be a kind of Labor day "watch-along".

I'm psyched.

Now, full disclosure: Realistically the event is going to be over with by the time you read these notes – unless you read SUPER fast. So... what we're going to do is put a full recording of the live stream up for anyone to see if they join after the event.

Again, this is any tier you join at... just a bonus for being a part of the family over there.

We're even having a poll to determine which film we watch. We've tried to keep them all a little British, or British vs American, for maximum humor. (Amy regularly does an Ellie accent, and is gradually teaching me some American, which is highly amusing. For her.)

The movies in the mix are:

The Full Monty,

Sherlock (TV show),

Four Weddings and a Funeral

Bridget Jones's Baby,

and Hot Fuzz.

<Michael Add: I suggest Hot Fuzz... Lot's of Hot Fuzz and Paul (about the alien).>

I've only seen two out of the five, so I'm looking forward to broadening my horizons!

If you'd like to check it out, here's the link to the poll.

https://www.patreon.com/posts/cast-your-vote-20894279

Kisses and the missing text generation

MA and I were talking about the back-matter layout of the new Nickie books. I was asking if the link to my fb page was still being included, simply because there is no Oz in this series to do the reminding before the author notes.

MA checked.

MA: Yep it goes in after you put 'e' and 'x'.

Ellie: (thinking for a moment) You mean 'Ex'? That's my initial and then a kiss.

MA: I thought a kiss was :-x... like in a face?

Ellie: I think you might have missed a generation of texting.

<Michael Add: Probably? I'm personally happy I've to emoticons in my repertoire. I'm almost 51 for @#@#'s sake.>

MA and his Self-Journal

MA was making some reference to his to-do list and it reminded me of his Tony Robbins calendar thingy. I asked him about it.

MA: I'm not using that anymore. I'm using that one you suggested.

Ellie: Panda?

MA: No, the Self-Journal.

Ellie: Oh great. That one is awesome. (I used to give them out at my business masterminds because they're so effective). How's it been for you?

MA: Yea, good. The one time I used it it helped.

Ellie: (Blink blink).

MA: *Shut up.*

<Michael Add: Apparently, 'shut up' (or the 'oh be quiet') doesn't extend to Author Notes.>

MA and (Time-)Travel

MA was in China or some place like that. We were chatting on slack to organize details for the various projects. Once we were done with the essentials I thought I better ask about his travels.

Ellie: so, how's the trip?

MA: Oh - trip is 'k' - I hate long flights and are on layover for 2 hours to continue to Beijing. Signing probably tonight. It's 6:30 AM right now here.

MA: Tuesday

MA: I WENT INTO THE FUTURE!

MA: Or is it Wednesday?

MA: Fuck, I don't know.

MA: Oh... Tuesday says my laptop

Ellie: hahhahaa #authornotes

John DeBlanc vs Nickie

For the keenly observant members of the Kurtherian family, you may have noticed that our character John

Deblanc has a strangely similar name to one of the gang: John DeBlanc!

How so?

Well, we like to honor our readers and helpers as much as possible... and last month John joined at the Patreon level where I said I'd name a character of him. He was psyched about it, and this was my first opportunity since he signed on. So that's how John Deblanc of Zuifra was named.

And with so many new series I'm in the process of launching won't just be in Michael's Kurtherian Universe that you can leave your legacy for readers. (And yes, at this stage you can probably choose. Just drop me a message in there).

If you're interested in this and scores of other perks, feel free to check out becoming a member here:

https://www.patreon.com/ellleighclarke

I'd love to connect with you over there!

Ok, so I've already used about two thirds of our back-matter allowance for this book, so I should probably let MA say something.

Thanks again for reading! You're the best.

Ellie x

Tabitha 03 ;-)
<<Ellie edit: Bwahahahahahahaha ^^^^ >>

First, THANK YOU for not only reading these stories but giving us a chance to crack at each other as well.

As you can tell, Ellie has been a bit busy there in Austin, and with her social media. I admire her ability to keep her stuff all in order since my social media is all over the place.

#Crapfood

So, during this conversation Ellie and I had on the phone yesterday? Two days ago? I think two days ago, she was commenting on her travels to Asia and how the only thing she had difficulty with was finding and being able to eat fresh food.

Now, my concern with coming to China was that I wouldn't be able to find ANY food I was going to want to eat. I was worried enough that I did research into the subject, and found out KFC was a big deal here in China, and if I was in larger cities, I'd probably be able to eat just fine.

And so I have.

I've had Japanese, buffets (international hotels seem to have these HUGE restaurants with food from a few different styles. I've noticed now in both Asia and previously in Europe, that Italian food is the "go to" choice for me) and I've eaten Chinese food at Lost Heaven in Shanghai (WONDERFUL!)

However, what I haven't tried to locate is anything remotely labeled fresh.

So, when Ellie was complaining (I suppose you could spin it as "commenting") that it wasn't easy to find fresh food, and all she could find was processed stuff, I retorted, "You mean that food I eat all the time?"

<<Ellie edit: Tee hee. If I recall correctly I was also expressing genuine concern about you being able to find non-native food. I'm always game for trying local cuisine (unless it's one of those weird delicacies like bugs or frogs legs, or sheep brains...) but I know you struggle with new stuff. That was where the conversation started. >>

Too many time zones

Ellie is on Central time in the USA, I'm on...HTFDIK in China (approximately 13 hours apart I think.) She has a weird sleep / non-sleep schedule and I'm never sure when is good to call her. I've decided it doesn't matter since whenever I try to call her, she's asleep.

<<Ellie edit: Bwahahahahahahaha. Not true! >>

BUT with her weird sleep schedule, I'm probably too

nice not calling her at midnight her time, (2:00 PM in the afternoon my time) and screwing up trying to reach her at 11:00 AM her time, 1:00 AM my time.

However, I usually get a ring back or a Slack comment within 30 minutes whenever I reach out. Sometimes I find out she is out with Amy (look out Austin!) and others she is in the middle of a nap. Because naps fuel her life. With such a screwed-up sleep schedule, that's how she copes.

I, on the other hand, am usually good with a night of sleep and one nap after a large lunch at Javier's (Aria Hotel). Here in China, I usually sleep from 9:30 pm to 3:30 AM – then wake up to work for a couple of hours while team members are up in the USA and then fall back for a nap before breakfast. I'm JUST getting into the groove to sleep longer, and I go home in three (3) days. Just in time to HATE MY LIFE adjusting to USA time.

I'm back one night in Vegas, then fly to Atlanta, Georgia (the state, not the country for you John Ringo fans) and visit DragonCon.

Hope I saw you there! (I'm flying home when this book is released.)

This book would be much later

If it wasn't for Ellie keeping me on track, and Natale Roberts helping me too, this book wouldn't be where it is (in front of you, being read.) I sincerely appreciate the Editors (Lynne's team) / Artist (Jeff-fa-fa) / JIT team / Jami and folks and everyone who has helped produce our stories, and this one in particular.

<<Ellie edit: Np, MA. I'm massively impressed that you've stayed on track with all the traveling and

schmoozing you've been up to. I'm also pleasantly surprised to have your *Author Notes* ahead of schedule. Well done, chap. Well done :) >>

If you liked these stories (or ANY author's stories) consider giving them a review, it helps our marketing for the next fan!

Just a note. If you happen to go to Shenzhen, China. The town isn't two gas stations and a single light, it's a city of about twelve million people. SURPRISE! (Also, it's a note for me to pay attention to the cities I'm going to visit and learning a bit about them before I jump on a train, not knowing where I'm going to end up.

Ad Aeternitatem,

Michael

BOOKS WRITTEN BY MICHAEL ANDERLE

For a complete list of books by Michael Anderle, please visit

www.lmbpn.com/ma-books/

All LMBPN Audiobooks are Available at Audible.com and iTunes

CLICK HERE TO SEE ALL LMBPN BOOKS ON AUDIBLE

CONNECT WITH THE AUTHORS

Ell Leigh Clarke Social Links

Join Ellie's Email List here
http://ellleighclarke.com/

Facebook
http://www.facebook.com/ellleighclarke/

Website
http://ellleighclarke.com/

Michael Anderle Social Links

Join the email list here:

http://kurtherianbooks.com/email-list/

Join the Facebook Group Here:

**https://www.
facebook.com/TheKurtherianGambitBooks/**